MOTORCYCLES AND MAGIC

JULIE L KRAMER

INFRINGEMENT,
INCLUDING
INFRINGEMENT
WITHOUT MONETARY
GAIN, IS INVESTIGATED
BY THE FBI AND IS
PUNISHABLE BY UP TO 5
YEARS IN PRISON AND A
FINE OF $250,000

Cover Design: Fantasia Covers

ONE

~

It's one thing to know that your mom left you. It's another to know that she left you a motorcycle and a curse.

I stared at the letter in my hands, trying to understand what I was reading. Mom hadn't been home for a few days, but I had figured that it was just another bout of her wanderlust, or a bounty that had gone sour and then she had needed to rest for a while. It wasn't like her not to contact me if something bad had happened, but we all had our off days, and I wouldn't have judged her if she had forgotten to call me; we would have laughed about it later and I would have chided her about remembering the important things, but then we would have moved on like nothing had happened. The letter in my hands told me that that wasn't the case at all.

I'm sorry. I can't explain, but I need to go away for a while, and I need you to not follow me. The bills are paid. Stay safe and I'll be back as soon as I can.

There was no signature, nor any kind of identifying marks, but it wasn't hard to figure out who it was from; Mom and I lived here alone, so it couldn't have been from anyone else, but that didn't make it any easier to figure out why she hadn't wanted to stay, nor why she had decided not to tell me before she left. Still, the fact that she hadn't signed it was enough of a problem. She never did that; she always signed her letters to me, even the notes that she left taped to the fridge or the bathroom counter. Her handwriting looked hurried, like she had been in too big of a hurry to write it that she had forgotten to sign it at the bottom, which wasn't like her. Her signature was one of the most distinctive things about her, and she was very proud of it. She had always taught me that signing in cursive, with my full name, was the only way to make a good impression: Renegade Emberley Moseley, with my huge R that dwindled into far smaller letters with each time and started tilting in about the middle of the word if I didn't have a line to write on. I knew her signature almost as well as I knew my own, because she had always drilled it into my head how important it was. For her to not sign such an important missive was strange, and it worried me. My hands had started to shake as I was staring at the note, my nose and eyes burning as tears loomed. I was not going to cry, not because I didn't want to, but because Mom wouldn't want me to. She had never tried to tell me that there was anything wrong with crying; she was a better mother than that, but that didn't mean that I hadn't learned from her. I couldn't remember the last time that I had seen her cry, and besides, it wouldn't help me anyway.

My knees were locked in place, but I carefully folded the note and shoved it into my pocket, trying not to think about it any more than I had to. I wanted to check the house for anything that she might have left behind, other than the obvious. If she had put enough thought into this that she had paid the bills for presumably months in advance, then it was unlikely that she hadn't thought to take at least some basic necessities with her, which meant that anything she had left behind could be almost as important as what she had taken with her. Or at least that was what I told myself. I had no idea what I was looking for, but I figured that I would know it when I saw it. Of course, that was easier said than done, and eventually I gave up and sprawled on the couch. It felt like giving up, but it was more like a tactical retreat.

Magic is easier to sense when you're familiar with it, the same way that you can recognize the footsteps or the perfume of someone that you spend a lot of time with. That's why I could sense the sudden spike of Mom's magic, enough to tear me from my funk. I flung my legs over the edge of the couch and padded through the house, using my own magic to track hers. When I was a kid, it had always been a game that Mom and I played, one that helped me to gain better control of my magic. We would hide throughout the house and leave messages for one another, messages that would appear at another time or another place. For me, the extent of my abilities was when I had made them pop up in the kitchen when I was hiding in the attic or something like that; it was like a magical version of playing hide and go seek, with a little bit of message-in-a-bottle flair thrown in. As I had gotten older it had been much easier, and I had often used the magical messages rather than my cell phone, if it was dead or there was no signal. All it took was a piece of paper, a pen, and a little bit of concentration. I could feel that same tiny spark of magic throughout the house now, in several different places, which meant that Mom hadn't just left one note for me. That, too, was strange, because Mom was a simple woman; she didn't mess around like that. If there was something that she wanted to say, then she would write it all down in one place, no matter how big the piece of paper was or how tiny her handwriting had to be in order to fit on it. So why hadn't she done that this time?

The bike in the garage is yours. I love you, and I know

that you'll take good care of it. It was always meant to be yours, when you graduated, but this time I won't be around to give it to you.

I swallowed hard, doing the math in my head for that. The fact that Mom didn't think she would be here for my graduation suggested that she was going to be gone for a long time. If not forever. And I couldn't let that happen.

I found another note in the attic, hidden in a pile of boxes. I coughed once, my eyes watering from all the dust that was moving around kicked up. Being up here killed my allergies, so I rarely came up here. Mom didn't either; she always said that there was nothing up here but the past, and she wasn't exactly eager to go back to that. Whenever she said that, she always looked a little wistful, and it made me think that she wasn't telling me everything that had happened when I was younger. I knew that my father wasn't exactly a great man, but she had never told me much about him. I never knew why she didn't want to share, but I thought she must have her own reasons. Unfortunately, right now it looked like her reasons were taking her away from me, and if that meant playing a magical game of hide and seek for yet another note, then so be it. Fine.

I found the next one in one of the old boxes, tied to a strange looking bracelet. It looked like it was made of both leather and silver, twisting together with a glittering black stone in the center. There was a spark of magic as I touched it, just enough to be painful, and I sucked on the tips of my fingers as I glared balefully at it, contemplating whether or not it was worth it to pick it up. Clearly Mom had intended for me to have it, or it was a serious coincidence that it happened to be stuck right there where the third note was. If she had meant for me to have it, then I would have appreciated it if she hadn't spelled it so that it tried to bite me when I picked it up, although I supposed I should be glad that she hadn't spelled it to literally bite me; she was a powerful witch and even if she wasn't the most skilled at spells like that, since she had more experience with battle spells because of her job, but she was still capable of doing some serious damage if she wanted to. I had no idea why she wouldn't want me to have the bracelet, and why she would have made the note appear so close to it if she hadn't wanted me to have it. Either that, or I was just reading way too much into this whole situation. I thought that might be a little more likely than Mom making such a huge mistake, so I carefully reached out again. I fully expected that it was going to shock me again, so when it didn't, I breathed a sigh of relief. There was a spark of magic that I recognized as Mom's, as if it were trying to recognize me, before everything went quiet again. I couldn't say that I blamed it for trying to make sure that I was the right person for the note, if that was what was happening. Honestly, that was the only reason that I could think of for it to be acting like this, not to mention the only reason for Mom to be leaving messages everywhere for me. She had left the one non-magical note in a place where I could very easily find it, and the rest I'd had to hunt for. But if I had to hunt for them, then that meant someone else had to as well. Now that I thought about it, that might have been the same thing that had happened with the bracelet and it's change of mind when it had shocked me the first time but not the second. The extra layer of protection had been put in place to make absolutely sure that the person who was reading the notes she had left for me was actually the person who was supposed to be reading it. It made sense, but that was just something else that scared me about this whole situation. The fact that Mom had made sure to put an extra layer of protection on some-thing as simple as a note to me meant there was more going on here than met the eye. I was swearing under my breath about the fact that she had decided not to let me in on any of whatever this situation was, because that would have been too easy. Part of me hoped that this whole situation was some sort of game, that I only had to find the last note and she would come swooping back in to give me a hug and praise on a job well done, but the longer I searched, the less I believed that.

I slipped out to the garage, keeping a wary eye out for any more magical surprises that Mom might have left for me. We had an outbuilding full of bikes that

Mom had restored, but the ones that she loved the most were in the attached garage, where they were always close by in case she needed to check on them. More than once I had caught her sneaking out here in the middle of the night, cleaning them up or polishing them, like using her hands to fix something that she loved was the only way that she could calm down enough to be happy. I had started doing the same thing when I was old enough to get my license. There were plenty of bikes in the garage, and Mom hadn't been very specific in her note. Maybe it was in case someone else found the note, or maybe it was just another example of Mom's annoying tendency to be vague, mysterious, and overly dramatic. Who knew?

Raising my flashlight, I squinted at the bikes. I couldn't see any signs of what bike Mom had meant for me to take, at least not right offhand. There were plenty of them and I knew which one I would have picked, but that didn't mean that that was the one that she would have picked for me; parents have this annoying tendency to worry about things like safety when they pick a vehicle for their kids, even if Mom was a little more easygoing in that department by letting me have a motorcycle in the first place. She had always stopped me from getting one of my own, even when I got my license, by saying that there were plenty of bikes for me to ride. Now it made me wonder if maybe she had been less worried about that and had instead been thinking of giving me one of her bikes this whole time. There was no way to know, but it hurt to think that she might have been preparing for this for so long and had never told me.

The beam of my flashlight caught something strange. It was just a shadow, but that was part of the problem. It was in a spot where there was nothing that would cast a shadow to match it, which I confirmed as I quickly did the math in my head, making sure that I wasn't just imagining things. I was afraid to move the light away from it in case it moved; yes, I was aware of how stupid that sounded, but when there was magic involved, I would rather not take my chances. Mom had already set a few magical traps that I had been able to either avoid or disarm, but something about this particular bit of dark magic didn't feel like something that Mom would have set up. It wasn't just that I couldn't sense her magic, but also that I couldn't sense any magic at all, yet I was still able to see it right in front of me. Cloaked magic was never a good sign, and I didn't want to take any chances. I was torn between moving closer to investigate it and backing away, because backing away seemed like the much better option, but unfortunately, that wasn't going to help me figure out what it was any sooner.

"My name is Renegade Mosley," I told the empty garage. I might have been self-conscious about talking to myself, but I wasn't talking to myself, something that was much easier to convince myself of when I could still see the magic. Mom had told me that the quickest way to make sure whether a spell was intended to do harm to me was by announcing my name.

If the spell didn't mean me any harm, then the magic in my name, and my voice, all the way down to my blood, then the spell would leave me be. If it did mean me harm, then at least I could get it out of the way, and I would rather know it upfront.

Wish granted. The shadow lunged at me with a sound that I could have only described as a bark, although I was more worried about what it looked like coming at my face than why it sounded like a dog from someone's afterlife. I dove for the ground and rolled, scrambling for magic to protect myself with. A burst flew from my fingers and slammed the dog in the chest, except not really. Slammed implied that it actually did some sort of damage to the dog, which was patently untrue; the light hit the dog in the chest and passed straight through without stopping, and neither the magic nor the dog seemed to notice that anything unusual had taken place. My magic splashed against the back wall and disintegrated, taking away the burst of light that it had brought with it as an added insult to injury.

"Come on, dude. For real?" I sighed and backed away, magic falling from my fingers as I kept a wary eye on the dog. I had no idea what it was, but I did know that it wasn't supposed to be here, and it shouldn't even have been able to step foot in the house. Mom had placed every kind of protection that she could manage on the house, even on the grass outside, and I had no idea how this monster had managed to get past all of those protections. Unfortunately, that didn't matter very much right now, because it was about to take a real chunk out of me right here and right now.

I shot another burst of magic at it, throwing all of my power at it in the hopes that it would do some good. The light passed through it again, but I could see that it did a little bit of damage, although I couldn't tell how much. I contemplated trying to find something out about it, but I had no idea how; it wasn't as if it was a person that I could interrogate, because I was going to be very surprised if it could speak, and that might have been the last straw of a really weird day. Someone had clearly sent it here for some reason, but I had no idea why. The only people who lived here were Mom and I, but she was gone, and the only thing I could think of was that this random demon dog had some sort of connection to her disappearance. It was possible that the two events were entirely unrelated, but somehow I doubted it; Mom had always taught me that there were no such things as coincidences, and a dog from way down under showing up on the same day that she decided to make like a rabbit did not seem qualified as something that wasn't connected to the other event.

I could feel myself slipping, running out of magic, but finally the dog yipped and slithered away. I didn't see where it went, nor how it disappeared; one minute it was there, standing in the dim light of the garage and seeming to glow from the inside out, then it was gone and had taken the glow of magic and shadow with it. I cautiously stepped toward the spot where it had disappeared, reaching out to poke the air with my hand. I know, I know, trying to poke the air to make sure that there isn't some demonic creature of shadow standing there was probably not the safest way to go about it, but there was no other way that I could think of to make sure that there was nothing else in the garage with me, other than using more of the magic that was barely hanging on as it was.

There wasn't, something that I was only sure of when I had searched the whole garage from top to bottom, with both my magic and a flashlight; my magic was still struggling, but I knew that I wouldn't feel better about it until I was able to use it to check, so I just sucked it up and did it. Only when I was sure did I step back into the house, lean my back against the wall, and slide slowly to the floor. It was only once I was back and safely on my own, for sure this time, that I realized that I was shaking, hard enough that slivers of magic curled from my fingers like sparkles of glitter. That was something that rarely ever happened with me, mostly because I was able to deal with my feelings better most of the time, not to mention that I absolutely refused to humiliate myself like that in public. Right now was one of the rare occasions that I was willing to let myself feel whatever I needed to feel, even if it made me look weak. There was no one else here to see, and since Mom had gone missing, I thought that I was able to look a little weak for a few minutes. Any teenager was entitled to a few minutes to figure out what they were feeling, something that even Mom would have agreed on.

And that was exactly what I did, allowing myself a good cry before I took a deep breath and swiped the tears away from my eyes. I had checked every inch of the house for whatever Mom had left me, and I was no closer to understanding what was going on now than I had been before.

I couldn't find any other notes, no matter how hard I pushed my magic, but of course I did still end up finding something, tucked beneath Mom's mattress of all places. I would have thought that she would have been smarter than trying to hide something in such an obvious place, but then again, it might have been because she had known that I would search here; whatever the reason, the circular logic wasn't making it any easier for me to focus. The small item was Mom's journal, wrapped carefully in a piece of cloth that had a faded logo on it, something that I doubted meant anything. Still, leaving her journal here was just another sign that something was wrong. She wrote in her journal every day, just to keep her thoughts fresh. I was hoping that something in her journal would tell me what I wanted to know, but a quick flip through of it showed me nothing that I didn't already know. The search had all been for nothing.

Which meant that I was going to do it all again, until I either figured something out or got too frustrated to continue. I jogged down the stairs to start in the kitchen again, then slowed once I reached the landing so that I could study the house. Mom might have tried to think of everything when she had taken off, but that didn't make it any easier to stay. There was no way that I was going to stay here in this empty house and worry about where she was and what she was doing. I couldn't guarantee that I would be able to find her, but I at least had to try.

~

I lowered my head as I rode by the police car that was stopped, instinctively slowing down, even though I wasn't speeding by that much. It was less about the fact that I was speeding than the fact that there was a cop at all. Of course, I had done some questionable things with Mom before, some things that were of questionable legality. I doubted that the police in whatever little backwater town this happened to be (I hadn't been paying attention to the sign when I rode by it, and the only reason I knew the town was small was because I was looking at it right now) watching out for little old me, since I was pretty sure that there were no active warrants out on me, but I also doubted that they would let it slide that I was a teenage girl on a motorcycle with no adult in sight. I hadn't been to school for a few weeks, and no doubt they were starting to get suspicious. True, I had tried with some excuses in the first few weeks, but there were only so many times that I could say that I was sick or that Mom couldn't come to the phone before they stopped believing me. I wasn't sure that they would stop me for truancy, but I was hoping not to find out. I also wasn't sure that I would ever be allowed to go back if I took off for this long, or that I wouldn't get in trouble when I did, but I was trying to think less about that and more about what was going on right now. Mom had disappeared, and that was the more immediate problem.

Don't get me wrong, I appreciated any clue that I could get as to Mom's whereabouts, but I would still have appreciated a little bit more warning before the spark of magic practically slammed me in the face, filling my vision with a bright light for the space of a few seconds. I flinched so hard that my bike skittered, the wheels screeching once before I was able to get it under control. There was a gas station down the road that looked like a perfectly appropriate place to stop, especially since the police were still behind me and I knew that they probably wouldn't follow me into a gas station unless they actually had a reason to. Besides, getting gas wasn't a bad idea, and it would give me a chance to track down where I had felt Mom's magic come from.

I might have been distracted by the burst of magic that had thrown itself in my face, but that didn't mean that I was blind. A boy ran out in front of me, not paying attention, and the wheels of my bike screeched as I tried to slow. Judging by his height, he was certainly old enough to know better than to run out like that, and I had no idea why he had done it in the first place. Not that it really mattered.

I yanked my helmet off, jerking my chin to get my sweaty hair out of my face. The boy looked entirely taken aback by the fact that I was a girl, but he was about to be much more surprised. Riding for hours at a time with nothing but road and trees to see didn't exactly put me in the greatest of moods, and neither did almost hitting someone because they weren't paying attention.

"Be careful!" I snapped. "You could have gotten hit." I didn't say that I was going to be the one who had hit him. That was relatively obvious because of the way I was acting, the fact that I had almost hit him, plus there was always the fact that there were plenty of other people who could have hit him if he kept acting the way he was. It was a matter of principle that he not act like an idiot in the middle of the street, not just because of me and my temporary distraction.

He cocked a dark eyebrow, leaning casually on the pump as I took out my wallet and passed over the cash so that he could pump my gas; he was wearing overalls with the logo of the gas station on them, or I probably would have stalked off without speaking another word to him. I had thought that there were no more gas stations that pumped gas for you, but of course I had been lucky enough to find one with an obnoxious attendant. I was trying to be careful with my cash because I had no idea how long I would have to make it stretch, but I also couldn't risk using any credit cards in case someone used it to track me. I knew it sounded paranoid, but that didn't mean that I was wrong. The next step was to figure out how to track down Mom's magic from here. Part of me was apologetic over the fact that I had almost hit him, but apparently my brain had decided to respond to guilt by getting angry at him. Immediately.

"Well, maybe if you had been paying attention, then you wouldn't have almost hit me." Our eyes locked for a second, and I straightened. I could sense that he had magic and for a terrible moment I thought that I had misread the magic in the air, that it was his and not Mom's, before I realized that that wasn't true; the magic was there, but his didn't feel the same. I couldn't quite put my finger on what kind of magic it was, but it didn't really matter; as long as it wasn't Mom's, then it didn't matter. There were plenty of people in the world who had magic, some specific and some general, like mine. I had no way of figuring out what kind of magic his was, but beyond simple curiosity, I didn't really care.

I took a deep breath, fully prepared to argue with him, then changed my mind. I didn't want to draw attention to myself any more than I had to by arguing with him, especially since he seemed like the type of person who would remember a face; I didn't want him to conveniently remember my face if the police started asking about me. That was the last thing I needed, so for right now, that meant curbing my attitude.

I jigged impatiently as I waited for him to finish with my bike. I could feel his eyes on me, but I refused to look at him, instead keeping my attention firmly on anything but him. Apparently something about me smelled like trouble to him, because he had no hesitation in telling me what he thought.

"So you're just going to roll into town and cause trouble, then?" I hadn't really done anything yet, or at least not anything that could be that troublesome, but apparently he had already made up his mind about me. I hesitated, unsure how to answer the question. It was a fair point, as much as I hated that it was true. I had come here for my mom, and if I happened to cause a little bit of trouble in the process of doing that, fine. I was fine with that. Mom might not exactly have encouraged me to cause trouble, because that was a bad parenting move no matter which angle that you looked at it from, but she had always told me that sometimes what other people called stirring up trouble was really just doing the right thing.

"Yeah, I guess so." I bent down into a crouch, my knees cracking as I settled next to the tires of my bike. Riding for such long distances always made me want to stretch my legs, but I didn't want it to seem like I was prancing around for this boy whose name I didn't know, since he seemed to think highly enough of himself already without me adding to that. Now that I was down here, I wasn't sure that I could get back up, so I twisted my head to look around, trying not to look like I was stuck because of my crap knees. There was another boy sitting in front of the store, long legs crossed as he read, and I found myself straightening up to study him a little more closely. I leaned back against my bike, ignoring the boy who had asked me a question in favor of looking at the other.

There was always something fascinating about watching someone read, especially when they were so engrossed in their book that they hardly remembered that the "real world" existed. He was curled up in a rocking chair at the front, his long legs crossed and one knee poking through a hole in his jeans. He held the book open with one hand and had the other up by his mouth, gently chewing on one of his nails. Normally that sort of thing irritated me, but he was so engrossed in his reading that I didn't think he noticed that he was chewing his nails. It was a habit that he probably didn't even know that he had, and I knew for a fact that I did the same thing when I read, mostly because I had once bit my nails until they bled when I was reading about a character's death in one of my favorite books. Part of me wanted to ask him what he was reading that was so interesting, but I hated to interrupt him when he looked so peaceful. Unfortunately, the other boy didn't have the same compunctions. He might not have interrupted the boy, but he certainly did interrupt me.

"Are you going to stay and stare at my brother all day, or is there something else that we can help you with?"

I waited a moment longer, partly so that I could irritate the one standing next to me and partly in the hopes that the other one would look up and meet my eyes. I didn't know what would happen if he did meet my eyes, but I would be more than happy to give it a shot, especially if he was as cute as he looked while he was reading. I couldn't see his face, but something about him made me think that he was cute, and that fact was only backed up by the fact that he was reading what looked to be a rather thick book; intelligence was attractive, at least in my opinion. When I realized that he wasn't going to look up, I swung my leg back over my bike and winked at the one who seemed so intent on challenging me, leaning forward on my bike with my arms on the handlebars and my foot on the kickstand. Maybe it was the fact that I was in a strangely better mood now that I had seen the other boy reading, which was probably the calmest thing that I had seen in days. Or maybe it was just like I felt like this boy was challenging me, and I couldn't say that I didn't like it. I looked him dead in the eye and kicked my bike to life, ignoring the money in his hand. I knew that it hadn't been the correct change, a few dollars over, but I was fine with him having the extra. I had been a little lean with my money lately, but as much fun as I was having pushing his buttons, I had better things to do than sit around here.

"I haven't decided yet." I winked and leaned away, checking the street before I rode out. He might have distracted me, but not enough that I was going to get hit trying to get out of here. Even as tired as I was, as exhausted as I was from the long ride, I was still curious about this town. I had never been in this town before and had no idea where I was going, but if there was one thing that I knew about my Mom, it was that the quickest way to find her was to look for trouble.

CHAPTER

THREE

~

Of course, I did manage to find trouble right away, because if there was one thing that I could do on my own, it was find trouble. It wasn't necessarily that I was tracking Mom's magic, but rather that I was able to find the place in town that she was most likely to have visited, which happened to be a biker bar. I would have thought that it would have been closer to the edge of town, since establishments like that tended not to get along very well with their neighbors, but it was firmly in the suburbs, with a gravel parking lot full of bikes and trikes. I stopped at the rear of the lot and pulled my helmet off, brushing my hair away from my face so that I could see better. I had lost the "scent" of Mom's magic at the gas station, maybe because she wasn't anywhere near here, or maybe because I had been too distracted by the boys at the gas station. Either way, I couldn't exactly bring myself to feel bad about it.

Other than my encounter with the boy at the gas station, and the one that I would have liked to have had with his brother, I hadn't met anyone in town. There were plenty of stares to go around, and that was just because I was riding a motorcycle; there would have been even more if they had seen that I was as young as I was, although it was possible that they were just admiring my bike. Going to a biker bar was probably the worst place in town to figure out what was happening in town, how the people of the town behaved, but I didn't have much of a choice. Besides, that was the place that Mom was most likely to be, so that was where I was going.

Unfortunately, that was easier said than done, especially when I wasn't actually old enough to be in the bar. I was torn between letting my hair down to hide my face and pulling it back to make myself look older, then decided on pulling it up in a ponytail. It was less about trying to look older, although I had always thought that I looked older with my hair pulled back, and more about me having a helmet head; at least with a ponytail, it was harder to see that. I doubted that they would try to I.D. me, at least if I was judging this place correctly, but I had a spare I.D. that had aged me up a few years. Surprisingly enough, Mom had been the one to get it for me, just in case I ever needed to bail her out of a bar or a club situation. Another questionable parenting choice, but she might have thought that I wouldn't want to abuse it because she had been the one to give it to me, and she was probably right about that. After all, it was no fun to use something that didn't have an element of danger to it.

There was a surprising amount of people in the bar, considering that it was in the middle of the day and I would have expected for people to be at work, but I was more surprised by the amount of magic that I could feel in here. It felt like the whole room was drowning in it, enough to make my skin prickle as I swallowed hard. I searched the room slowly, trying to make sure that the source of Mom's magic hadn't come from here. Of course, it was probably wishful thinking to think that I would find her magic in the first place I looked, but I still had to check. With all the magic here, it was hard for me to sort through what was what and make a decision as to which of them mattered to me and which ones didn't, which was harder than it sounded.

Mom's magic wasn't here, but I followed the brightest flame of magic to the back of the building, sliding through a side door with a backward glance to make sure that there was no one was following me. At first I thought that there was nothing back here, other than a few pieces of old sheet metal and some twisted pipe. Then I heard a soft growl and froze.

My heart pounded as I flashed back to the darkness of the garage, but this time, as dark as the dog was, the shadow it threw onto the ground was very real. A black and tan Doberman climbed to its feet, white fangs glistening as she snarled; at least I thought it was a she, if the feminine head told me anything, because that was about all I could see right now, probably since my eyes were zoomed in on her fangs at the moment. The chain hooked to the collar around her neck rattled as she stood, prowling to her feet. I backed away, magic glistening on my fingers, but not fast enough; she lunged, and I yelled as her sharp teeth sank into my arm, gouging so deeply that blood and magic mixed on the surface of my pale skin.

I froze, unable to decide what to do. Her teeth were already sunk deep into my arm, so it wasn't like I had anything to lose; as long as neither of us moved, we were fine, but this situation wasn't one that could last forever, not that I would want it to anyway. I didn't want to hurt the dog, but I also didn't want to yank my arm away and hurt myself in the process. I had never seen something injure me so badly that I could see the magic as well as my blood welling up from my blood; I actually hadn't even known that was possible. I couldn't say that I was exactly ecstatic to find out this particular way. I stared down at my arm, alarmed to see the magic swimming in the dark liquid. Did animals that got a taste for magic want more of it? I wasn't sure if that was blood or magic, but either way, this was a situation that I hadn't been prepared for.

The dog's ears perked, her deep brown eyes curious as she watched me. No doubt she was confused as to why I wasn't screaming and trying to pull away from her, which was probably the most common reaction to her. It was a sad life for a dog to have, but as far as being a guard dog went, she was doing a bang up job so far. I didn't want to tear myself up trying to get away from her, but it wasn't like I didn't deserve it; I was at a bar I had no right to be at, and I was technically trespassing in the back of the building, where I had even less right to be at. Still, I wasn't exactly happy to have a dog taking a chunk out of my arm, and I was even less happy when the back door creaked open, accompanied by the sizzle of magic and cigarette smoke.

I wrinkled my nose, but I didn't think it was too wise to make too big of a deal about the disgusting smell; that was the sort of thing that was best thought about privately, not complained about when I was doing something that I shouldn't have been. I turned slowly, facing a man with a huge beard and a long mane of hair. There were tattoos running down his beefy arms, arms that definitely looked strong enough to hurt someone; actually, he looked like he could have popped a watermelon with his bare hands, and even though I couldn't tell what the tattoos were, somehow I doubted that they were unicorns and fluffy bunny rabbits. He looked less than enthused by the fact that I was out here, not that I could blame him. I was definitely trespassing, and I was starting to regret having followed the magic.

"Hi," I said awkwardly. As if it irritated her, the dog took another bite, her jaws tightening on my arm. I winced. There had only been a few seconds where she hadn't had her teeth embedded in my arm, a blessed relief that I had barely even noticed, and I was kicking myself for not getting away while I had the chance. I should have yanked my arm away instead of standing here like an idiot, but I was too scared. I could admit that to myself, at the very least.

"What are you doing back here?" he asked. "This is private property."

I hesitated, unsure of what to say. There was really no good way to answer this question. I didn't want to lie, but I also didn't want to admit that I had been looking for magic. If I did, then he would know that I was aware of magic, and for most people that meant I was a threat. I especially didn't want him to know that I was looking for my mother, because that was information that he didn't need to know about me. It might not matter to him, but any information that I gave away about myself was something that could be used against me, and considering that I was currently trespassing on private property and I could sense the magic in the air, I wasn't eager to give him any more of a leg up over me than he already had.

I might as well tell the truth, or at least a version of it; that was normally the best way to go. "I was looking for someone. I thought she might be out here." Not technically a lie, because I had thought she might be near here, even if she wasn't exactly back here. I was looking for someone, and by saying that rather than saying that I was looking for someone, he might think that I wasn't a thief, which was the truth. I wasn't here to steal anything. I just wanted to find my mom. The dog had finally let go, and I cradled my arm against my side, trying to ignore the blood that was leaking through my shirt. The liquid was warm and sticky on my stomach, enough that I could feel it when I moved my arm in order to settle it more firmly against my body.

The man clearly didn't care what I had said; either he knew that I was lying, or he was seriously offended that I was trespassing, because again I felt the sizzle of magic, although this time it was clearly a threat, rather than just something that had happened to be happening at that particular moment. My own magic reared its head in response, striking back like a snake, not that it did much good. It was overwhelming, and I hunched over, startled by how much force he was exerting with the magic. A few others came out, adding to the magic pushing against me. And I might have been able to handle that, if it had just been magic that they were striking at me with, but when fists and feet entered the equation, I couldn't quite make it. I tried to fight back, but there was only so much that I could do. My whole body was lit up with agony, blood trickling down my face. I curled up in a ball and tried to push back, but the combined effects of magic and physical violence were enough to keep me down. Eventually it was all I could do to protect my head, and even that was too hard by the end.

I groaned as two of the men lifted me by the arms, my injured ribs protesting as they dragged me through a hole in the fence and into an alley nearby. It had been mid afternoon when I had stepped into the bar, and as hard as it was seeing through my bruised eyes, it looked like it was approaching dusk; I didn't think the beating had lasted that long, but magic had a tendency to make things kind of strange. I retreated into my magic, trying to shrink away from the pain as they dumped me unceremoniously in the fetal position in the alley. I curled up on my side, retreating as far back into my magic as I could manage in the hopes that it would help me heal faster, but that didn't mean that I couldn't see the feet walking toward me through the slits of my half-closed eyes. I could feel myself fading from consciousness as hands, far gentler than the ones that had handled me before, lifted me from the filthy ground and carried me away. My head fell back, and the ground blurred as I faded into unconsciousness.

FOUR

I could taste blood and magic in my mouth, like I had been kissing someone with a tongue ring; to be fair, I wasn't exactly sure where the magic came into that scenario, but whatever. It tasted metallic and sharp, and I swallowed hard, fighting the urge to open my eyes because I knew it was going to hurt something fierce. Still, waiting around for it to stop hurting meant it was going to be a hot minute before I could even get up, and I wasn't patient enough for that. So I slowly cracked my eyes open, even if it did feel like someone was jamming a needle into my eye when the light hit them.

"Where am I? And who are you?" My voice sounded strained, which surprised me; my throat was the only thing about me that didn't hurt. Only after I said it did I recognize the two boys from the gas station, sitting near the bed, or rather cot, that I was stretched out on. The rude one was further away, seated on a workbench with his legs pulled up, while the one that had been reading was closer, sitting on a stool with a concerned expression.

"I'm Cade. And this is my brother, Liam." I tried to sit up, wincing. My arm might have been in its socket, but it was a close thing, and I was fairly certain that it hadn't been when I had zonked out. I remembered the dog, and the bar, and the beatdown I'd gotten after I'd gone somewhere that I shouldn't have. I'd always thought that I had a hard head, but apparently not hard enough. I sat up slowly, wincing as I raised a hand to my head. Both of the boys shifted forward like they were going to stop me, but I swung my feet over the side of the cot. It wasn't the first time I had woken up somewhere I wasn't supposed to be, usually a library, a bar, or a hospital, but it was the first time I had woken up in what looked to be a mechanic's shop. There were pieces of what looked like parts everywhere; a few loose screws rolled under my foot, which made me realize that my boots were gone.

"Renegade. Where am I?" And what was I doing here? They seemed to be pretty decent, at least judging by the way they looked. I would have been able to tell that they were brothers even if they hadn't told me.

They both had blond hair and blue eyes, striking royal blue that shone in the light. It was a serious contrast to my own pale hair and dark eyes, chocolate brown.

My jacket was gone, as well as my boots. I glanced around, instinctively crunching in tighter on myself. It wasn't because of the fact that I was wearing a crop top and had several inches of my abs showing, because I had glorious abs; I was decently good looking, and the only reason I knew that was because of how hard I had worked to gain confidence, since good genes will only get you so far. The reason I was cringing in on myself was because everything hurt, and my natural reaction when I was hurt, like most, was to make myself as small as I could. I was tall, so I couldn't make myself too terribly small, but I was definitely going to give it my best shot. It wasn't the first time that I had ever gotten into a fight, but it was the first time that I had been beat down that way. It had been a hard lesson to learn, but even as hard as I had gotten conked on the head, I had still learned it. And believe me, I was never going to forget it, either.

"Ernest's garage. We live here. We brought you here when we saw you get tossed out of the bar."

My eyes narrowed. Other than hurting, I didn't think that anything had happened while I was unconscious, but that didn't mean that they had brought me here out of the goodness of their heart. Still, even hurting as badly as I did, I was pretty sure that I could take them both on, and maybe even win. Then again, that same confidence had been what had gotten me in trouble in the first place, so if there was

"And why would you do that?"

The brothers looked at each other and shrugged. One had longer hair than the other, but other than that, they looked almost exactly the same. The one with the longer hair, just long enough to brush his chin, grinned at me slyly. He had a circle of black around his irises, and his eyes sparked at me. "Because any enemy of the Pit Vipers is a friend of ours." I opened my mouth to protest that I wasn't their enemy, then snapped it shut so hard that my jaw clicked. Given the beat down they had just given me, and the fact that I had gone there looking for my missing mother, I thought it was pretty safe to say that I was an enemy of the Pit Vipers. I hadn't even known what the group was called, but given that they were the only ones that I had had any sort of encounter with, other than the one with the boy sitting in front of me, it only made sense; honestly, the name fit them pretty well, better than I would have liked. I hadn't found my mom, or any indication that she had been here, but that didn't mean that I was ready to give up just yet. All I could sense when I slipped into my magic was that there was something wrong, something dangerous, and that only confirmed what I had already known from her note and the fact that she had left me high and dry.

As much as I wanted to, I couldn't argue with that logic. My bike was parked in the corner of the garage, next to the rest of them that seemed to be in various states of disrepair, but I was just glad that it was here instead of parked outside of the bar that I had been tossed out of. Literally. Despite the fact that Mom had said in her note that it was mine and always was intended to have been, I was only just now starting to think of it as mine instead of hers, and even that didn't happen all the time; it just depended on the way that I happened to be thinking at the time. I didn't know how they had gotten it here. I was just hoping that they hadn't done anything sketchy to get it here, but what I didn't know wouldn't hurt me. Probably. Maybe.

I was still holding my arm tightly against my side, wincing as I reached for my boots. I hadn't seen them at first, but I wanted to get myself together as much as I could, even if it hurt like the dickens to do it. My jacket was neatly folded over the top of the desk chair that Cade was sitting on. Both of the brothers stared at me, slack jawed, and I stopped what I was doing for a moment to roll my eyes at them; secretly I was glad for the excuse to hold still for a moment, especially

since every move I made made my body beg for mercy. I straightened up, my boots in front of me. I wanted to put them on, but I just couldn't bring myself to do it just yet.

"Can I help you with something?"

Liam recovered first, with the same sly grin. He leaned back in his chair, tossing his thick hair back. I was somewhat jealous of the mane that he had going on. Not that there was anything wrong with my hair, which was a pretty thick mane itself, but somehow it just made me mad when guys had hair like that; they didn't always appreciate it like females did. But judging by the way Liam looked, actually the way both of them looked, they took their looks seriously enough that I needn't have worried about that. Liam was attractive and he knew it, but I didn't get that same vibe from Cade.

"We just thought you might need to rest. You know, since you did just get your butt handed to you."

I made a face. I was a decent martial artist, maybe even good, but I had just learned the hard way that numbers can overwhelm even the best of fighters, especially if magic was involved. Still, I had more leads to check out. Well, not really, since my one lead had been following the magic that I had lost, but I was desperate for any excuse to get out of here and recover some of my wounded pride, not to mention keep going through my mom's journey. I had been sleeping in some seedy places for the last few days on my way here, and not many of that had enough light for me to read the journal by. The fact that Mom had left her journal told me more than anything else that she was in trouble, and I was just hoping that there was something in the journal that would tell me where I could find her or how I could help her.

"I'm aware of that, thank you. And thank you for your help." I leaned down, and kept wincing, trying not to sound like I was a balloon with the air being let out of it. Mom would have smacked me silly if I hadn't at least thanked them, and I was thankful for what they had done; I wasn't being sarcastic when I said that. I regretted that I had walked in there like an idiot, but I was already starting to feel better, and the fact that I'd gotten my butt handed to me once wasn't going to stop me from going back if that was what it took to find Mom. I vaguely remembered something about the definition of insanity being doing the same thing over and over again, but I was willing to overlook that if it got me where I wanted to go.

Cade's long fingers tapped my ankle gently, and he helped me slide into my boots. His hands were soft as he guided my feet into the soft leather, then pulled the zipper up the side, careful not to pinch my skin. I nodded gratefully, accepting his help to stand. The best thing about magic was that it helped me heal abnormally fast, although I didn't heal as fast as some other magical creatures. My arm was still sore, but the bruises were fading, and the scrape on my cheek had faded to a manageable scratch. There was probably no internal bleeding, and even if there had been, I was pretty sure that it would have healed by now. Or, at the very least, I would have noticed it by now. Even better, I was pretty sure that I wasn't concussed, which meant that it was safe for me to ride out of here and find a place to stay. Unfortunately, that would be a lot easier if I actually had somewhere to stay.

I sighed and rubbed my forehead. My pride was already in tatters, so I may as well throw it to the wind and ask the boys if they knew of somewhere to stay.

"Look, I know we barely know each other, since this is the first time we've met, but I appreciate what you did. Now I need one more favor." Both boys pricked up. Cade looked like a puppy, while Liam looked more like a boxer sensing an opening. That was something that I could understand, but it highlighted the difference between the two of them. As far as he was concerned, I was admitting weakness, and that was something that he could take advantage of. "Any suggestions of where I could stay the night?" I had been sleeping on my bike since I had left home, which was exhausting, and it wasn't like I was having the best of all night's sleep when I did. I was constantly exhausted, and I was still dodging the cops.

Truancy officers were the real deal, and they didn't particularly care about whether or not my mom was gone. I had tried to talk to the police when she had first gone missing, but I had given up fairly quickly, for several reasons. I didn't know that none of them cared about her disappearance; despite my differences with the law in the past, I still firmly believed that there were good and bad people in every profession, and this was no different. Unfortunately, that made it all the more urgent that I not screw things up by getting caught now, and that meant that I needed to find somewhere to stay.

Sure, there were plenty of hotels in town, but that didn't mean much. First of all, just because there were hotels, that didn't mean that they would let me check in; for the hotels that had bars, I wasn't even twenty one, and I actually wasn't even eighteen yet. I might have the money to check in, but that didn't mean that they were going to look at me and not realize that I was a little younger than I said I was. Actually, I had no idea what the minimum age was to check into a hotel, but I was pretty sure I wasn't there just yet. Plus, there was always the chance that they would see through whatever lie I had come up with and decide that they were going to take a more careful look at what I was saying, which would pretty much be a disaster at this point. Home hadn't been seen to in more than a week, although I had had the good sense to have the mail held at the post office so that there wasn't a massive pile of mail on the front porch that told every robber in the neighborhood that their sticky fingers would be well put to use on the house. Of course, with all the magic that was around the house, there was plenty of protection in place, but that still didn't make me worry any less about what amounted to nearly all of my worldly possessions, other than the clothes on my back and a few on my bike. I had already made up my mind that I wasn't going home until I found Mom, and if that meant that I needed to put aside my worries about whether or not our house was going to get robbed, then it looked like I was just going to have faith that the magic would hold.

I had also placed a strong spell around the house, one that allowed animals in but kept anyone out. We had a large porch in the back, and there was always food and water there for any animal that happened to need it, which was something that Mom had always insisted on. Maybe it was her way of making sure that I had some sort of animal presence in my life since I wasn't allowed pets, or maybe she was a bigger softie than people gave her credit for, with her motorcycle collection and her many tattoos. Either way, it didn't really matter, because I had tried to keep up her wishes as best as I could. Other than staying home like she had asked me to, of course. That was out of bounds for the moment.

The boys glanced at each other. I could tell that they weren't sure what to say, not that I could blame them. They didn't know me, but they had just saved me after I had gotten my butt handed to me. They probably felt a little bit responsible for me, which was the precise opposite of what I wanted them to feel. I had done what Mom would have wanted me to and thanked them for their help, but I was ready to move on and free myself from being any more in their debt. Right now, that meant finding a place to heal and rest up so that I could continue with my search for Mom. I wasn't sure how I was going to find a way to pay them back for saving me, but I would find a way to do that before I left town. I didn't like being in anyone's debt.

Whatever the glance between the boys said, they had come to the same conclusion, because Liam nodded reluctantly. He looked far less excited about whatever prospect they were considering than Cade, but I didn't think that was uncommon; I had barely known them for a combined total of like an hour, but already I could tell that he was a little more emotional than his brother, or perhaps enthusiastic would have been a better word.

"You can stay here for the night." Cade was the one who had made the offer, which made me realize that that must have been what the look that had passed between them had been about.

"Or as long as you want," Liam added. I cocked an eyebrow, startled that he was the one that had extended the invitation for a longer stay rather than his brother, until he dropped the other shoe. "But only if you tell us why you're here."

Of course it couldn't be that easy. I kicked myself inwardly for thinking that I could just hitch a free ride and get away with it that easily. Still, I did owe them, and they were the best option that I had for a place to stay, not to mention someone that could help me with what I needed. There were some things that only the locals knew, and I was certainly not a local. Out of all of the people that I had met in town, also known as no one, these two were the only ones that I might even consider trusting enough to ask about my mom. I was going to have to ask someone if I wanted to get any more information on Mom, and it might as well be them.

"Fine. We'll trade. You tell me what I walked into at the bar, and I'll tell you why I'm here." It was a terrible compromise, and I felt a little guilty about playing them like this, but not bad enough to change my mind. I wanted to know what had happened at the bar. Yes, I had been trespassing, but that shouldn't have warranted the butt kicking I got, which had told me just how much my martial arts training didn't mean when they could overwhelm me with magic. I had never been trained to withstand that kind of magical assault, as good of a teacher as Mom had been, and I was really feeling that gap in knowledge right about now. Then again, she hadn't expected me to be in the field in the first place, so that might have been why she hadn't bothered to teach me. True, she might have thought that not teaching me that was the only way to make sure that I didn't do it; sometimes, making sure that kids had to learn their lesson the hard way was the only way to make sure that the kids stayed safe. She should have known me better than that.

Liam rolled his eyes, leaning forward as a challenge. "We took care of you, at great personal risk, I might add. I think you owe us more than we owe you." I opened my mouth to protest, more than happy to argue with him because that was all that I had the energy to do. Before I could get a word out, Cade smacked his brother on the back of the head, which produced a very satisfying sound.

The brothers glared at one another, and every inch of my body ached as I tensed, expecting the two of them to start brawling right here. It wasn't my job to get between the two of them if they did start fighting, nor did I think I would be able to do much good if I did. I felt weak as a kitten right now, and as much as I wanted to haul off and slap one of them, that was about the best that I could do. "What is the matter with you? She's had a hard enough day without you making it worse , and she doesn't owe us anything. We helped her because it was the right thing to do." Cade may have been the quieter of the two, and definitely the more polite if our short experience had taught me anything, but he was standing up to his brother like a champ. I partly hoped that he hadn't, because it made me feel guilty enough that I felt like I had to tell them what I was doing here.

"My mother disappeared. I came here to find her." Obviously I hadn't managed to do that, but I figured they were smart enough to figure out what the problem was with that. I had gone to the bar in order to find more information about where she was going, but there was only so much that I could have found out in the short amount of time that I had been there. In fact, that made me wonder what the two of them had been doing there. They hadn't been at the bar that I had seen, but that didn't necessarily mean that they weren't there; they weren't old enough to be at that bar, but neither was I, so it was a moot point. Had they shown up at the bar just in time to save me? It seemed unlikely, but so did the fact that I had followed the "scent" of Mom's magic to a town that I could find no sign that she had ever been to.

Liam's face softened. He might have been the one that challenged me about why I was here, but he was also the one that reached out toward me. He was further away from me than his brother, but that didn't stop him from crawling down from his perch and offering me a packet of trail mix as a peace offering. His eyes had softened, and again I saw that glint of magic in his eyes. I could also see it when I looked at Cade, but the glint was muted, as if he was less powerful. Cade might have been the calmer and more approachable of the two brothers, but there was something about Liam that made me think that there was more to him than I had thought before. The fact that I could see the glint of magic in their eyes meant that they were seriously powerful, even if I couldn't tell right offhand what their powers were.

"As you can tell by the fact that we live in a garage, we don't exactly have the most stable lifestyle in the world. So we get it. You can stay here, and we'll help you find your mom." Both Cade and I glanced at Liam in shock. A flush appeared on his high cheekbones, but he crossed his arms, clearly too stubborn to take back what he had said. I was suddenly glad that I had told them about my mother.

Warm tears pricked at my eyes and I hurriedly lowered my head, gently stroking my fingers through my hair to hide the pending tears from the boys. I had been wrong; my eyes didn't hurt either, but I was pretty sure that the salt in my tears wasn't going to do huge favors for the cuts on my face. Beyond that, I refused to cry in front of them, as much as I might have wanted to. It might have been embarrassment or frustration, but either way, it wasn't happening. I was just so grateful that I finally had told someone about Mom, when I had spent the past few weeks constantly being afraid and worried about Mom. All of that frustration was coming out right now.

"Thank you for that. But I haven't forgotten our deal. What did I walk into with the Pit Vipers?" It was a strange name for a small town biker gang, but the reek of magic and the massive dog in the back, not to mention their willingness to beat me up, told me they weren't exactly small time. Maybe Mom coming here had something to do with them, or maybe it didn't, but there was no way that I was going to let them get away with whatever they were doing. I couldn't see a problem and then walk away from it like that.

The boys glanced at each other. Cade nudged Liam, who rolled his eyes and explained. "We don't know exactly what's happening for sure, but we are pretty sure that there is some kind of blackmail involved. The Pit Vipers have everyone in town, from the mayor on down, eating out of their hands. No idea how or why." He shrugged eloquently, and I frowned. I hadn't seen any evidence of wrongdoing other than the reek of magic, which meant I had no proof that the Pit Vipers were doing anything seedy. Neither did the boys, but it seemed that all of us shared the same bad feelings about them, a fact that I filed away for later.

Me raising my hand to brush my fingers through my hair had reminded me of the wound on my arm, the one where the dog had decided to take a chunk out of my wrist. I lowered my arm, studying the white bandage wrapped around my wrist. Cade moved slowly toward me, sinking onto the cot next to me like he was afraid he was going to startle me. I appreciated the effort, but I was so exhausted and in so much pain that I doubted I could have panicked.

Liam whistled softly. "You've got a pretty impressive bite there. Who took a chunk out of you?" I made a face at him, but he genuinely didn't seem like he was making fun of me, which was the only reason that I didn't make a rude gesture at him and ignore him entirely.

I quickly explained how I had tried to follow Mom's magic and had ended up at the business end of a seriously aggressive dog, one that was apparently not the slightest bit bothered by my magic. Most dogs, or any other animal, would have been affected by it, but not this one. Another thing that I couldn't understand was why that dog had looked so similar to the one that had tried to take me out in the garage. Well, that was purely a guess, because I hadn't seen any sort of corporeal form of the dog in the garage, but a large and aggressive shape seemed to fit with the flesh and bone one that I had just encountered. I hadn't seen anything like it since, although of course I had kept an eye out. Probably to the point of being obsessive, if I was going to be honest. The closest that I could figure was that it was a spirit or some sort of familiar, but I hadn't met anyone before or since that had a familiar like that, especially not someone that would have a vested interest in trying to kill me. Not at the time, anyway. Any member of the Pit Vipers would probably have happily taken a chunk out of me at the moment, but I hadn't even met them yet when the incident in the garage had taken place. I had no idea who would have wanted to hurt me so badly, but there was a nagging sense in the back of my mind that the dog, or whatever manner of creature it had actually been, hadn't been after me at all. It made no sense that something or someone would decide to take their anger out on me right after my mother had run off into the sunset. The two events might have been unrelated, but somehow I doubted it.

"Fine. Do you have any idea where your mom would be? Any idea at all."

I shook my head. The only idea that I had was to follow Mom's magic here, and that clearly hadn't turned out very well. It was a dead end, and I had no idea where to go next. The only place where I had felt even close to finding Mom was at the bar, but I had clearly ruined my chance at that. The longer I thought about it, though, the more that I refused to give up on that idea. That was my last chance, and I wasn't going to let something like a beat down put me off Mom's trail.

"Okay. That makes sense. Do you have a plan?"

I hadn't until that very moment, but now that they asked me, I had to have an answer. It was a matter of pride, but that didn't mean that it was a good plan. That would have been asking too much from the situation. "Yes. I'm going to go back to the bar and break in tonight."

~

Both of the boys stared at me, and I cracked a slow grin, unable to contain something nearing glee. If nothing else, then at least I had managed to make them stop and stare at me for a moment, and it would all have been worth it just for their expressions. Despite the seriousness of the situation, not to mention how absolutely crazy what had just come out of my mouth had been, I still wanted to snicker at how shocked they were; maybe it was because I had been able to come up with a plan so quickly, or maybe it was because of how shockingly bad that plan actually was, but either way, I still thought that it was funny. I was fully aware of how crazy my plan was, but I didn't have a better one.

The biggest worry that I had was about the dog, who had already proven that she was more than capable of taking a chunk out of me. My arm was still throbbing, which was strange. Most wounds healed relatively quickly with magic, and although there were a few exceptions, I hadn't expected a dog bite to be one of them. Maybe she was a familiar, but I couldn't believe that anyone would have left their familiar outside, chained up like that. I would never have done that, not that I had ever considered finding my own familiar. There were pros and cons to it, but it had just never been the right time. Still, I couldn't believe that someone would treat their familiar like that, but if she wasn't a familiar, then I had no idea why the bite was taking so long to heal. Then again, there were exceptions to every rule, and maybe animal bites took longer to heal no matter what animal they were from. I had never really been around animals as a child, so I didn't exactly have any experience to fall back on.

Cade was the one who spoke first, already shaking his head and clearly completely taken aback by my suggestion. "You can't. That's suicide. You barely got out of there alive the first time."

True. I was unfortunately fully aware of that, but that didn't mean that it was going to change my mind. The smart thing to do would have been to stay home, at the house that I had grown up with, where Mom had done her best to arrange everything so that I didn't have to worry about anything. I was fully aware of that too, but I had also known that when I had looked at that fact and then made the decision to entirely ignore the smart thing to do. Instead, I had been dodging truancy cops and scrounging up cash for weeks, trying to make sure that I could find Mom and not get in trouble in the process. Doing the stupid thing was in my genes, and that was exactly what I was going to tell Mom if she tried to get on my case about me coming after her; she should have known that there was no way that I was going to stay put like a good little girl. She had taught me to always do what I thought was right, even if it wasn't necessarily the smartest thing to do, or the safest. If anything, this whole situation was her fault. I wasn't angry, but I was frustrated, sad, and worried. I couldn't imagine how she felt, but I wasn't exactly looking forward to a long heart to heart chat about our feelings when I finally caught up with her. At this point, I would have been more than happy if I had been able to find her, or even a trace of her magic at all.

Liam nodded. As usual, he seemed to have taken up residence on any surface that was not meant for sitting, like a cat. He was curled up on the table, spinning a wrench between his long fingers in the same way that a drummer would spin a drumstick. "Look, as much as I'm happy to help with any stupid plan, especially one that my brother doesn't agree with, he's right. This isn't safe. And besides, how do you know that you'll even be able to find anything there?"

I didn't. That was the simplest answer, but it wasn't the one that they wanted to hear. It was the only chance I had, and some small, stubbornly stupid part of me was determined to get back at them for beating me up. I had always known that I wasn't infallible, but to get such a jarring reminder was harsh to say the least. Maybe that was why I was so determined to find something there. At least that way I wouldn't have gotten my butt handed to me for nothing. Besides, Mom's magic had led me to this town, and that was the only place that I had felt even a shred of magic here in town so far. I couldn't shake the feeling that the two were somehow connected.

As bad as the plan was, the boys couldn't come up with a better one, so they reluctantly set out to help me. I wasn't sure whether or not any of the Pit Vipers would recognize my bike, so we all drove separately on some of the bikes that were laying around the bar, then headed inside. The boys and I sat at the bar, baseball caps pulled low. Both of the boys were locals, so anyone from around here would recognize them. I wasn't from around here, but anyone who had been at the bar the other day for my lovely show of getting dragged through and tossed out on my butt would recognize me. My hair was pulled up and hidden under the cap, so hopefully between that and the fact that I was partially healed, I was hoping that no one would recognize me. My entire body felt tender, and it protested when I moved. I was nursing a glass of cool water, and every few minutes I leaned my cheek against it, trying to ease the shiner that was in full form against my eye. It would have helped if there was more ice in it, but at the moment, I was happy for any relief that I could get.

Dimly, just above the din of the bar, I could hear the tv in the corner playing the local news. I might not have paid attention to it if I hadn't seen something that caught my attention: me.

Apparently I wasn't the only one who was paying attention to the tv, nor the only one who could recognize my face, because both of the boys swung their heads to look at me. I nudged Cade with my foot and he hurriedly looked away, but Liam, who was sitting nearer to me, leaned over to speak to me in a low voice. If ever there was a time to not draw attention to myself, then this was it, but apparently he didn't care about that. Not that I was surprised.

"You told us that you were a truant. You didn't tell us that you were a bank robber."

I'm sorry, do what now? I squinted at the tv screen, trying to read the information scrolling across the bottom. I had thought that it was strange that the authorities would put my picture on the news just for missing a few days of school, but I had never skipped out of school for this long before; I didn't know how this whole thing worked. But Liam was right. The information below the picture was about a bank robber, one that very clearly had my face. As much as I wanted to stay and find more information on whatever the heck was going on here, I was all too aware of the offer of a reward on the screen as well. Nearly everyone in this bar would have turned me over for the bounty, and I wasn't even sure that the boys wouldn't if it came down to it. I could feel the eyes on me, making my skin crawl. It was time to leave. I carefully slid a wad of cash across the counter to pay for our drinks, then pulled my hat lower and headed for the door; I didn't say anything to the boys, but I could hear the soft scuff of their shoes as they climbed off their stools and followed me to the door. Every step toward the door, my shoulders were tense, waiting for someone to say something to me or stop me. It was only when the three of us were back to our bikes and kicking them to life did I finally relax. We left in a hurry, but the short ride back to the garage wasn't enough to help me work out some of my frustration. Even pacing around the garage wasn't helping. It felt like the walls were closing in, even if my brain was still struggling to comprehend what exactly was happening in my mess of a life right now.

"I don't get it. What's the problem here?" I rolled my eyes, trying not to be too irritated with the boys. It was a perfectly logical question, and the fact that they hadn't turned me over to the cops yet was a mark of how loyal they were, despite the fact that we barely knew each other. It wasn't their fault that I wasn't patient enough to stop and explain things to them, but this girl, whoever she was, wasn't me. For one thing, I could see that she was a tad shorter than me, but it probably wasn't enough to make anyone else wonder; the only reason that I did was because I knew how tall I was, and standing next to the bank counter gave me a good idea of how tall she was. We had been watching the footage over and over again on our phones, but there were only two things that I noticed were amiss with the girl no matter how many times I watched it. My height, and one other thing.

"Toss me that wrench." It was a lot easier to show them than to tell them, especially since they didn't know me well enough to know that I was telling the truth. Still, the fact that these two boys who barely knew me, and had certainly seen me in a compromising position, didn't seem to be entertaining the thought that I was a bank robber for one second. If they were anyone else, I might have been insulted that my attempt at cultivating an image as a bad girl hadn't worked, but since it was the brothers, I was willing to let it slide.

I sent a silent thank you to anyone that was listening that it was Cade who picked the wrench up to toss it to me, and it was slow enough that I was able to catch it without trouble; still, my sore arm gave a twinge of protest, which was precisely why I was glad that it hadn't been Liam, because he absolutely would have tossed it at my head without blinking an eye. Not to be rude or intentionally cruel by jolting my injured arm, but because he didn't know what he was doing if he wasn't making a nuisance of himself. Did he wake up every morning and choose chaos, or was that just something that happened to him every time he made a choice? Who knew?

Cade still looked confused, and Liam rolled his eyes and tapped the picture on his phone to enlarge it, shoving it in his brother's face, so close that he had to lean back to see it. "She's right handed, and the person in the photo is holding the gun in their left hand." It was a pretty decent match for my looks and my clothing, but there were things to pick out that would warn anyone who knew me that I wasn't the one who had done this. Unfortunately, no one in this town knew me, and this was the one time that I regretted not having made more of an impact here. At least then I would have had someone to vouch for me, other than the boys. I didn't even know Ernest, despite the fact that I was staying in his garage. If past experience had taught me anything, it was that people only heard what they wanted to hear, and hearing that it wasn't me from three teenagers wasn't something that would be on their radar. It wouldn't work, mostly because when teenagers said something, it tended to go in one ear and out the other, at least where adults were concerned.

I dropped my head into my hands and groaned, muffling the sound in my palms; if I could have screamed without the boys thinking that I was absolutely off my nut, then I would have. As if it wasn't hard enough to find Mom now, adding the potential of being arrested for armed robbery was going to make it even harder. I would have to figure out what had happened to make me such a target for a conspiracy like this. Other than that, I would have to find Mom and clear my name. No biggie, right? Somehow I couldn't shake the feeling that the bikers at the bar had something to do with this, or at least knew someone who did. That was the only thing that made sense, especially since they were the only ones that I had angered lately. But for real? Pulling a stunt like this? That was just so beyond the pale I couldn't even wrap my head around it.

"I'll have to go back to the bar again." It was the last thing that I wanted to do. I found it mildly ironic that that bar was the one place in town that I should have wanted to avoid like the plague, and yet I had been there more than almost anywhere else. Still, if they knew something that I could use to clear my name, then I needed to know about it.

"No!" Both of the boys all but yelled it at me, both of them scrambling to their feet to block the door so that I couldn't walk out. Despite how different they were, I was both surprised and impressed by how well they had worked together to stop me, since it was almost seamless. "We can't stop you from going, but you need to figure out what you're doing before you go."

"What is there for me to figure out?" I asked. It was a genuine question, even if it did sound like I was being a smart aleck. The bar was the only place that I could think of where I might find some information, and the boys weren't going to stop me from going if that was what it took. Not that they could have, even if they had wanted to.

The boys glanced at one another. Clearly their instinct had told them that they should stop me, but they hadn't gotten any further than that, which meant that they didn't have an argument to stop me. Finally they both sighed. Cade was the one who spoke, while Liam retreated, looking every inch like the petulant child that he was acting. If I hadn't known any better, then I would have thought that he actually cared about me.

"Fine. But we're going to be your backup."

CHAPTER

SIX

I took a deep breath, facing the rest of the bar and trying not to think about all the ways that this could go terribly wrong. "My name is Renegade Mosley. And I'll only say this once: I didn't come here for a fight, but I want my mother, and I want my dog back." Of course, I was well aware of the fact that neither of those things were going to happen, but that was part of the reason that I had burst in here like this, because it certainly got their attention; Mom was who knew where, and the dog was very much not mine, but me raising such a stink about them was definitely going to raise some hackles. I resisted the urge to cross my arms. Mom had been a good fighter, and years of martial arts training had taught me that crossing my arms was never a good thing.Crossing your arms meant that you wouldn't be able to fight without yanking your arms apart, and those few seconds would be more than enough to get me in trouble. All I needed to do was distract them for long enough to think that I was gone for good. I didn't particularly want to get my butt handed to me again, but if I had to lose a little pride, then that was fine.

I wasn't sure that they wouldn't start a bar brawl in here, but I was counting on the fact that they would take me out back. Of course, everyone in this bar had probably been in a fight more than once, but I at least hoped that they wouldn't beat me up in here, because that was a situation that I wouldn't be able to control in the slightest. I didn't struggle as two of them grabbed my arms, dragging me through the same door that they had dragged me back through before. My feet dragged, and I resisted the urge to drag my heels. I didn't need to, and the only reason that I would even want to was just to be a jerk. Not that I was above that, but I had bigger fish to fry.

I counted quickly and fought down a smirk. There were only three of them. The others had stayed inside, clearly confident that these three could handle me. What they hadn't counted on was the fact that I was mostly healed and my magic was ready, willing, and able. They were about to be seriously surprised.

I was pretty sure that there was some long, complex

spell that would knock them out, but I had never been taught to do that, and besides, I had never been one for long, complex spells anyway. Instead, I did something that was much more aligned with my quick and dirty style of magic: I lashed out with my magic as hard as I could, which was the equivalent of getting kicked in the head, and knocked them all out just as quickly. I hadn't been able to pull that stunt the other night because there had been too many of them, and by the time I had pulled myself together enough to think about this, then it had been too difficult for me to focus enough to raise this kind of magic against them, something that I was still kicking myself for.

It wouldn't last for long, but I didn't need long, just enough to check out some of the other buildings back here, just in case there was something here that could lead me to Mom. I glanced around one last time, making sure that the only people around were the ones that I had knocked out with my spell. The dog was still out here, but she only watched, and did nothing to suggest that she was going to try to either take another chunk out of my arm or try to raise the alarm, both of which I appreciated. Still, I kept a wary eye on her as I crept around the sheds, peeking in the windows to see what I could see. Most of it was just junk, random things that had been collected and stored in the sheds for safe keeping, until my eye caught the motorcycle shining in the back. Normally that wouldn't have been enough to raise the alarm, especially considering that this was a biker bar and there were more bikes in the parking lot out front than probably anywhere else in the county, but this one was definitely special. That bike was one of Mom's favorites, and the lovingly restored classic stuck out among the other bikes like a diamond in a bed of sapphires. All shiny and valuable in their own right, but yet clearly different.

I wobbled, barely able to keep my balance on the top of the trash can that I was standing on. I was tall, but it wasn't exactly easy to peek into the windows of the shed like this. The whole thing was set at a weird angle, which didn't make it any easier to see. Once I had my feet safely on the ground I checked the front door, whistling softly through my teeth when I saw that it was securely locked. Not that I had expected anything else. Besides, even if I could have figured out how to get in here, there was no way that I would be able to ride the bike out of here; there were fences all around me, and it wasn't like I would be able to toss it over the fence like a soccer ball. No, the mystery of the missing bike would have to be solved later, and certainly not right now, when the bikers were starting to rouse; I had known that the burst of magic wouldn't give me much time, but still. Dang, dude. A few more minutes would have been nice.

No one would question what had happened to me, especially since they would no doubt make up a story about how they had gotten rid of me to save face. There was no way that the three of them would admit to anyone that I had knocked them out cold, but I wasn't going to stick around to see how they reacted to waking up like this. I headed for the fence, stopped by a soft whine. I paused, looking at the dog. Deep brown eyes stared at me, and I could feel her begging me to take her with me. It was too dangerous, not to mention stupid, but who was I to say no? Before she had bitten me, but I had no fear that the same thing was going to happen this time. I could feel a tether of magic stretching between us, and it didn't feel like it wasn't going to snap anytime soon. Whatever had happened when she had taken a bite out of my arm, it wasn't going anywhere anytime soon.

"I'll be back later. I promise." I meant it, enough that my magic rebounded in my chest, and I flinched. My magic normally only reacted that way when I lied, but I wasn't lying this time. It was the absolute truth, and even the dog seemed to know it, because she whined softly and lowered her head to the ground, watching me as I hurried away, trying not to look back. If I stayed for much longer, then I was going to get myself in trouble.

Hours later, I hopped the fence, leaning precariously on the pointy wood so that I didn't jump straight into a trash can or something equally awful on the other side. There was a soft growl from the black dog, although her ears pricked when I crept closer, a hand against my lips. To a human being that would have meant that she should be quiet, and I had the sneaking suspicion that this dog was smarter than most people. The growls immediately faded to a more manageable level; I felt like the only reason that she was even growling at all was because she had a reputation to uphold, even if it would have hurt my feelings if she had kept growling when she saw that it was me. The chain attached to her spiked collar dragged on the ground, rattling as she took a few steps forward. There was a padlock on it, and I swore under my breath as I picked it up. The key was snapped off in the lock, which meant that I couldn't even pick the lock. I could have made short work of the lock if I had been able to pick it, but since I couldn't, it looked like it was going to be the hard way. I had no idea who had decided to snap the key off in the lock; it was a jerk move if it had been done on purpose, but if it hadn't been on purpose, then I would have thought that there was someone around here who could have cut it off. But noooo, that would have been much too easy, and that couldn't happen in my life.

I straightened up, my eyes straining in the darkness as I searched for something that I could use to snap the lock or the chain. I was working by the dim light of the one working streetlight, which was halfway down the block, because I didn't dare use a flashlight in case one of the bikers inside the bar saw it and came out to investigate the light. There were enough guns, knives, and chains in that particular place to make me want to stay at least a city away from it, but there was no way that I was going to leave a beautiful dog like this chained out in the dark, especially with brutes like this. True, she had taken a pretty good chunk out of my arm, but I didn't blame her for that; she was just doing what she had been taught to do, which was protect the stolen property, and right now that included my mother's bike. Mom had had several bikes, all of them as lovingly restored as the one she had left me, and I couldn't imagine that she would part with one for no good reason. If it was here, then that meant that they had done something to her to get it, but it also might mean that she was still around here somewhere. Hopefully not hurt, but I would happily take just alive. Hurt, I could deal with. Dead...

I wasn't even going to go there. I couldn't think about that right now. Right now the mission at hand was to free the dog, which would get harder and harder the longer I was here. Every moment that I was here would mean that we were a moment closer to me being caught.

I bent down, searching for anything that I could use to get rid of the lock. My fingers found a long, slender pipe, and I carefully wedged it into the lock, the muscles in my arms straining as I pried it open. After a few seconds of pressure, the lock snapped and fell away, with me cringing at the noise that it made, my shoulders hunched as I looked back toward the door to make sure that no one had heard. If they had, then I had no doubt that they would have come running out like their pants were on fire. I breathed a deep sigh of relief after a few seconds had passed and it seemed like no one was any the wiser. The dog woofed softly, gripping the chain in her mouth, then trotted behind me as we both headed for the fence. Holding the chain was a smart move, considering that if she hadn't, the chain would have dragged on the ground and made even more noise than me snapping the lock off. Apparently the dog was smarter than me, because she had thought of it and I hadn't.

Now the same problem faced us as had faced me earlier, with the bike. There was no way that I was going to be able to lift her over the fence, and I couldn't think of another way for her to get out. I climbed up, crawling over trash cans and the various piles of other nasty things that I didn't want to think about, then paused to look back at her. She paused for a moment, her ears pricked. If I hadn't known any better, than I would have thought that she was studying the path that I had used, trying to come up with one of her own that would allow her to get up here with me.

I wasn't sure that she used the same path I had, but it turned out not to matter at all. In a few bounds she had cleared the fence, holding her chain in her jaws the entire time so that it didn't rattle. The second her paws touched the ground she turned back, waiting for me as if I were the one that was holding her up, not the one who had masterminded the escape in the first place.

"The nerve of some...dogs." I was muttering under my breath as I finished getting down from the fence, although I was all too aware that it was far less graceful than the way she had done it. I hesitated before I reached for the chain, wondering if I should hold onto it just to make sure that she didn't take off, but she didn't seem inclined to let go if it, and I certainly wasn't inclined to try to reach into her jaws and take it from her; I valued my life, and my fingers, too much for that. On the plus side, she didn't seem the slightest bit inclined to not follow me back to the garage, so at least there was that. The last thing that I needed was some kind of devil dog taking off in the middle of nowhere, because it wouldn't take the bikers long to realize that their captive pooch was gone, and I had serious doubts that I wouldn't be on the top of the list of people that they would blame. I also wasn't going to be the one to chase her down in the middle of the night, so for right now, I was just happy that she was willing to stick with me.

Thankfully the two of us made it back to the garage

with little issue, where the boys were waiting. There were a few plates of food on the table, and I snagged a piece of sausage for me and one for the dog with a mumbled thanks. They were both staring at me, so I chose to talk to the dog for the moment. I hadn't told them where I was going, mostly because I had known that they would protest at yet another occasion of stupidity on my part. I was unfortunately well aware of that, but, on the plus side, at least I hadn't actually gone into the bar this time. Yes, I had been on the property, but I was pretty sure that this didn't count.

"You need a name," I mused. Her ears pricked straight up, which somehow made her even cuter. True, she was built like some kind of warrior goddess in canine form, and I was kind of happy about that; I liked that about her. I wondered what had made her change her mind about me, because there was little doubt that she had also been a willing participant in this little game between us. Yes, I would have been more than willing to go back and get her, even if she hadn't whined at me, but she had. It was clear that she had played a part in this, not to mention the fact that she wouldn't have come with me if she hadn't wanted to. There was no way that I could have made her do anything that she didn't want to do. Either she had been bored, or she had decided that it was love at first bite. Who knew?

"Any ideas, boy wonders?" Both of the boys were

chowing down, but they were still watching the dog like she had more than one head, which I definitely would have noticed, even if I did like her a little more than I might have admitted at first. Then again, they had both seen the chunk that she had taken out of me to start with, so they were probably thinking about that when they looked at her. Not that I blamed them, because it was hard to forget for me too. But if I could get over it, then I had no doubt that they wouldn't be far behind.

Both of them shook their heads, clearly too focused on their food and ignoring the dog to come up with something. I rolled my eyes. Chickens. They couldn't ignore her forever, nor did I think that she was going to let them. She deserved a name that was just as scary and strong as she was. There were plenty of names that fit that description, but I had always wanted to have a dog, which meant picking a name for the one I did have, or at least the one that I had a chance to pick a name for, was of the utmost importance. It had to be the perfect name for her, because I might never get this chance again, and I wasn't going to squander this opportunity.

"How about Boudicca?" Her eyes pricked and her tongue lolled as she tilted her head, like she was deep in thought. It was the name of a warrior queen, which fit her just fine. "Boo for short."

That seemed to clinch it. She barked once and licked

my hand gently, then stretched out, mournfully eyeing the piles of food on the table. Somehow I doubted that she had been starved, because she was sleek and lean, but that didn't mean that she couldn't be hungry. She was a large dog, and it must have been hard for her to be so well behaved when it came down to having all this food all around her. I picked up a few pieces of meat and placed them on the floor for her, making a mental note to thank the boys, and Ernest, and get them some groceries as soon as things calmed down. Mom had always taught me that I should never owe anyone anything, and that was exactly what it would be if I didn't at least try to help out around here. It was the right thing to do, and just because she wasn't here, that didn't mean that I had forgotten everything she had taught me.

All throughout the night, even keeping up conversation with the boys and getting to know our new friend Boo, my head still wasn't quite in what I was doing at the moment, mostly because I was looking forward to what I was going to do later. I needed to head back to the bar one more time, just to make sure that I hadn't missed anything. This time I was going alone, less because I didn't want any help and more because I didn't want the boys to worry. With the bar closed down, I wouldn't have to worry about anyone being at the bar, and therefore no one would object to me taking a quick look around.

Or, at least, that was what I had told myself when I was picking the lock to the bar, keeping my eyes and ears peeled to make sure that there was no alarm that would trigger anything, whether magical or otherwise. I didn't want to take the chance that I would get arrested, and I definitely didn't want to chance that someone would stumble upon me while I was searching for some of Mom's stuff. Perhaps that was why I froze like a deer in the headlights when a man in a dark suit glanced up, along with just as many bikers as there had been in the bar when it had actually been open. My magic made a sound that was somewhat akin to a squeak; at least, I hoped it was my magic, and not a noise that I had made out loud, because I would absolutely die of embarrassment if that was the case. Then again, considering the glare that was currently pointed at me, that might have been the less painful way to go. I should have just backed out and at least tried to pretend that I wasn't breaking in, even though that was exactly what I was doing, and any idiot would be able to see that; as stupid as they acted, they still weren't stupid enough to buy that I wasn't doing something shady. All of that ran through my brain as I stared at the man in the dark jacket, my brain whirling as I tried to understand what I was seeing. It wasn't that I didn't know who he was, because I did, and I would have been able to recognize him anywhere. That didn't give me any more of a clue as to what he would be doing here, and somehow, I doubted that I was going to get much of an answer from him, especially with all of his friends around here. Then again, he had never been very forthcoming with answers in the past, so why would I expect it from him now?

"Dad?"

CHAPTER

SEVEN

∾

As expected, our little family reunion didn't exactly go as planned, mostly because Dad was a jerk and nothing good could happen when he was around. I had always known that, but being here, in a shady bar in the middle of the night, didn't exactly put him up for a Dad of the year award. I could feel the bruises forming on my upper arms, but I wasn't struggling at the moment; I had already figured out that I wasn't going to be able to brute force my way out of this, and I wasn't dumb enough to waste all of my energy when there was no chance of getting away. Right now I was more concerned with the fact that my father was here. I hadn't seen him in years, and now my mom disappeared and someone tried to frame me for a crime that would put me squarely on the naughty list for the law? Somehow I didn't think that was a coincidence.

"Now look what I found." The door of the bar slammed into the wall so hard that it rattled the neon clock, almost as hard as the floor rattled when Cade fell to his knees, shoved into the bar by a man that may also have been a gorilla; he was so large, and so hairy, that I couldn't have confidently placed a bet on either outcome.

I did my best not to let my feelings show, although I wanted to roll my eyes. Dad would be able to sense that there was something between us, or at least that we knew each other, but in order to minimize the damage, I needed to make sure that they interacted as little as possible. For right now, that meant getting Cade out of here before he said or did anything stupid.

"Let him go, Dad." I hated calling him Dad, but if that was what it took to get him to let Cade walk out of here, then I was fine with that. I'd get down on my knees and beg if that was what it took. Actually, Dad would probably like that; it would feed his already-massive ego. "He's got nothing to do with this."

Cade shook his head stubbornly. "I'm not leaving without you." There were a couple of wolf-whistles and laughs from the rest of the bikers, but it didn't matter much. What may or may not have been between us was none of their business, and they didn't get an opinion.

I rolled my eyes, drawing myself up to my full height. There were some pretty large people in this room, but I was plenty tall enough to hold my own. If there was one thing that I could pretend to be, it was tougher than I really was. "I'll be fine. Dad and I have a little catching up to do, but before that, how about we make this interesting?" I knew that I was making a show, and that was the plan. Gangs like this wouldn't care if I was my father's daughter, but they would care if I could act just like he did. I shrugged free of the men holding me; they were so startled that there was no resistance, which was exactly what I had expected. That had also been part of the reason that I hadn't struggled before, because then it would make them lower their guard, which was exactly what I had been counting on. There was also the small matter that I had been staring at my dad like a slack-jawed idiot for a good few seconds, but I was going to pretend that that hadn't happened and act like there was some sort of plan in place, even when that plan was dubious at best.

I stalked forward, chin tilted up as I squared off with my father. I might have inherited my mother's sense of right and wrong, but I could put on a show like my father, even if that's all it was: a show. I hadn't known him that well as a child since I was too young to remember him, but I did know what Mom had told me, and I did know that my instincts were telling me to act like the biggest jerk I could, because that was the only thing that he might understand. "I'll make you a deal. If I can beat you in a game of pool, Cade gets to walk out of here, and you and I talk. Privately." As desperate as I was to find Mom, I also knew that I wasn't going to get everything that I wanted, especially based on a game of pool. Dad might be willing to let Cade go just because I had been brave enough to challenge him to a game of pool, but he wasn't going to tell me where Mom was. That was going to require a little more work.

Dad tossed me one of the pool cues and I snatched it out of the air, swinging around so that I was holding it properly. Dad had taught me to play when I was younger, which was one of my only memories of him and probably should have warned me about what our relationship would be like, but Mom had taught me to cheat. If I was good enough to slip it past him, or even good enough to make him respect me, then I had a chance.

It was a slow, smooth game. It had been years since I had played, and even longer since I had played someone as good as him. I was starting to regret challenging him, but I leaned over the table, concentrating on the colorful balls. The next time that he leaned over the table to take his shot, I called on my magic.

Fighting always made my magic sleepy, like a warrior that had had her full of battle. I hadn't fought yet today, so there was plenty of magic right there at my fingertips. It didn't take much to make the eight ball swerve into the corner pocket instead of the one he had aimed for, just a breath of magic. He hesitated for a moment, as if he was going to protest that he hadn't lost, but that wasn't the way to make his people believe that he was in control. If he admitted that I had been the one to use the magic to cheat, then he would have had to admit that he couldn't control it, and me. Cade was the one thing in this situation that I couldn't control, but I was doing my best to ignore him until I had things taken care of. I knew how my father would think, and even though it was a gamble, I was pretty sure that it was still going to pay off.

"Fine. Your boyfriend is more than welcome to leave," he bowed at the waist, his hand stretching toward the door, and there were a few chuckles from everyone. It was a strangely courtly gesture, but any sincerity that there might have been was completely overridden by the sarcasm that it was dripping with. Cade wasn't my boyfriend, but now wasn't the time to tell anyone that, because him being something to me was the only protection that he had here, and I wasn't about to take that away from him. Still, I had to hand it to Dad. He knew exactly how to turn the situation to his advantage, making it seem as if he had planned this all along.

"I'm not leaving," Cade insisted stubbornly. He was smart enough to realize that he was very much in danger since he had decided to follow me here, but apparently he was more loyal than smart, because he was ignoring the danger he was in for me. It was sweet, but this was not the time for it. This was the first time that I wished that it had been Liam instead of Cade, because Liam would have had no problem getting out of here to save his hide. I didn't blame him for that; everyone was who they were, and I was the stubborn kind who stuck around and stuck my nose in where it didn't belong. Liam was the wily one who got while the getting was good, and apparently Cade was the one who somehow thought that I needed his help. I was never one to turn down a backup, except right now. It wasn't safe for him here, and I hadn't gone through the trouble of getting my dad to let him go only to have him insist on staying right in the thick of things.

I grabbed Cade's arm, dragging him toward the door. We were about the same height, but I had the advantage of surprise on my side. He clearly hadn't expected me to grab him, so he went along with it; I was glad, because I didn't want to hurt him, but he did need to leave. "Make like a ghost and vanish," I hissed in his ear. I shoved him out the door, then jammed the lock home so that he couldn't come back in. Places like this didn't lock from the outside; they locked from the inside, because the worst elements in town were inside, not out. I wasn't dumb enough to let any of them know that I was nervous being stuck in here by myself, but I did allow myself a moment to breathe deeply and try not to pound my fist into the wall before I turned back. At least now that Cade was gone, I would be able to focus on finding out more about where Mom was, or even if she had been here in the first place. Somehow I doubted it, if Dad was somehow here, because the two of them hated one another with a passion that I couldn't even begin to understand. Then again, I did know that if she had been anywhere near here, then he would have known about it; he may have been a nuisance, but he was a good guy to keep track of everyone who was in town.

"Dad, can we talk? Privately? " There was a soft chuckle that rose up from everyone in the bar, but I ignored it. I wasn't going to let them change my mind or sway me from learning what I could from this.

He nodded, motioning for me to follow him into the back of the bar. I hesitated for a moment, unsure of whether or not to follow him. I didn't trust him, but it wasn't as if I had a choice. And besides, it was a heck of a lot better than standing out here to have a conversation in front of all these people.

"So what are you doing here?" He asked without preamble, motioning for me to sit down. Which I didn't, because I didn't trust him at all, and sitting down while he stayed standing felt like showing my belly. Instead, I crossed my arms and tried not to start yelling, letting my magic reach out a little, feeling around as much as I could without allowing him to feel that I was fishing for something. I had no idea how his magic worked, since I had never given it a chance when I was younger; I had been too young to use mine when he was at home, and by the time that I was old enough to be in control of my magic, he was already gone. It had just been Mom and I, which made things both harder and easier at the same time. Still, I figured that it was probably better to have no father figure at all than to have one that would mess me up as badly as he no doubt would have.

Like right now, when the magic felt very strange. I frowned, not quite understanding what I was feeling. As far as I could tell, there was no trace of Mom's magic here, nor any indication that she had ever been here in person. Instead, it felt just like the note, as if she had intentionally left a trail here. This magic was something that made no sense, especially when one considered that I wasn't supposed to be following her; she had explicitly told me not to, and she'd had no way of knowing that I would completely ignore what she had told me to do. If not me, then who had she thought would be following her? As near as I could tell, she had let a trail lead here, so that whoever was able to track her magic would know where to look. But look for what? Other than me getting beaten up here, I had no proof that there was anything sketchy going on here, just like I had no proof that they had anything to do with the armed robbery that was currently staining my somewhat-good name at the moment. I had a sneaking suspicion that they had something to do with it, but until I had proof, all I had were questions.

There was a soft knock at the door and Dad called for the person to come in. I straightened up and frowned at him, somewhat offended that he would decide to let someone in here while we were in the middle of a conversation. True, it wasn't much of a conversation because he was an absolute wall when it came to talking about my mom, but I had expected that. I couldn't be sure that anything would be different if I had a few more minutes with him, but now we would never know. Since he had decided that someone else got to crash our short lived conversation, the only one that we'd had in years. To say that I was miffed was an understatement.

"Who's this?" I asked doubtfully, looking at the girl. There was something about her that I didn't trust, something that made her hard to focus on and look at. Maybe it was because she looked a little like me, or maybe it was because of how close she was to my father, but I didn't trust her as far as I could throw her, which wasn't far at all. It was like looking into a funhouse mirror: similar, but not the same.

"This is Lou. She's a witch, like you. I think you would like one another. After all, the two of you are very similar." He chuckled softly and motioned at her. I tilted my head warily, not sure what he meant by that and not sure that I liked it, either. There were quite a few things out there that I would not trust my father with, and another girl my age, a young witch, was right at the top of the list. As I watched in shock she transformed, her body twisting and shaping so that she was staring at me through my own eyes. If I hadn't been looking at her, I would never have believed what I was seeing. It was like I had a twin, although I knew full well that I didn't. She wasn't just a chameleon. She was a shapeshifter, but more importantly, unless I was totally misreading why Dad had made her transform in front of me, then she was the one who had pretended to be me in the bank robbery.

"It was you." It was more of a statement than a question, but she still nodded. Unlike anyone else with sense or maybe a bit of common decency, she didn't have the slightest bit of remorse on her face, as if it didn't matter to her at all that she had implicated someone else in a capital crime. Nor the people that had been in the bank, who had no doubt been absolutely terrified. She didn't seem to care at all, and it made me furious. "Why?"

She looked at Dad, who took over for her, even though she hadn't spoken a word this whole time. "It's something that we do here at the bar. If we think that someone can be useful, then we make sure that they have the chance to work with us, even if we have to blackmail them a little to help them see the opportunity that it presents."

I rolled my eyes. Only my father could manage to make blackmailing someone seem like it was for their own good. "So what about me? Did you just decide that I was a good option for blackmail when your guys beat me up, or was it just a way to welcome your daughter to town?" I growled. As much as it hurt my pride, there was no point in me lying to him about the peeps here at this bar handing me my butt on a silver platter, because I had no doubt that he already knew about it. Still, that didn't make it any easier to admit it, especially in front of this strange girl, who seemed to be doing her best to seem like the badder, scarier version of me. Not that that would take much, because I wasn't exactly the scariest person in town.

Dad nodded. Like Lou, he didn't have the slightest bit of remorse for what he had done to me; it seemed that as far as he was concerned, the fact that I was his only daughter meant nothing to him beyond the fact that he could use me for his own personal gains. I knew I shouldn't have been surprised, but it still hurt. "Yes. I knew that we could use a powerful young witch like you, but I also knew that you wouldn't exactly be excited to see your dear old dad."

I snorted. "You're right about that. You were a trash father." He wasn't my anything, and he certainly wasn't someone that I would have considered working for if I'd had a choice; he was right about that much. Lou moved toward me and, before I could do much more than look at her, she had raised her hand and delivered a stinging slap to the side of my face. I gasped, my hand flying up to rest against my cheek. It was warm, like any other slap would have made it, but when I took my hand away, there was a fine trickle of blood between my fingers. There was no ring that I could see, nor anything else that might have cut me, but there was still very clearly blood on my face. Maybe she had scratched me, not that the how really mattered as much as the fact that she had done it at all. I had wanted to punch someone since I had walked into the bar, and she was rapidly climbing the long list of people I was willing to take a swing at.

"How dare you speak to him that way?" she spat. I felt the same way about her, and I was already moving forward when Dad stepped between us. We both had magic, and so did he, which was how he managed to keep us away from each other when every part of my body was thrilling at the chance to give her a taste of her own medicine. Either she was crazy, brainwashed, or both. I of all people knew just how convincing my father could be, enough that he could make any bad decision seem like it was a perfectly logical choice, but that didn't make it any easier to know that he had managed to bully or bribe this girl into committing crimes for him, even if she had been wearing my face while she had done it. I was angry at them both, but right now, he was the one that was holding me back.

"What about Mom?" By now I could pretty much tell that he hadn't had anything to do with her coming here, at least if my magic was to be believed, but I still wanted to ask, just in case. Even if that meant that I was wasting my time here, I wasn't going to leave until I got a clear answer, even if it wasn't the one that I wanted to hear. Of course, I already knew that he only did things for his own gain, and she would have used him being here to his advantage if he had been able to.

He shook his head. "I don't have a clue where your mother is, but she's not here. I had nothing to do with her disappearance, or whatever else may have happened to her." I didn't like the way that he said that, but right now, he was right. I had no idea what had happened to her, and there was a very good chance that I wasn't going to know anytime soon, especially if I kept wasting my time on him. It was time for me to leave while the getting was good. I shot a filthy glare back at Lou, just to make sure that my feelings were clear. She shifted forward again and for a second I thought that my father wouldn't be fast enough to get between us and I would actually get a chance to punch her, but no such luck. Dad shook his head and Lou backed off immediately, leaving me to head out the door of the bar with a combination of relief and disappointment. Apparently I had wanted to punch someone even more than I thought I had. Oops.

As it turned out, as cool tempered as Cade was, he still didn't appreciate being sent out of the bar the way that I had done to him. I couldn't exactly blame him, since I probably would have slapped anyone that would have dared to treat me the way that I had treated him, so I sat down and waited for his temper to burn out. I deserved every word that he threw at me, and I stayed curled up on the table, waiting for him to finish so that I could tell the two of them what my father had told me, as well as about our new friend. Boo was curled up against my side, her head in my lap, and was unleashing a soft, constant growl that never wavered in depth or pitch as long as the boys were looking at me, or rather, as long as Cade was yelling at me. It was a clear warning, but neither of us thought that Cade was actually going to hurt me. Still, it made me feel better to know that someone was on my side. I guessed that was part of the joy of having a familiar. No matter how many people ganged up on you or how angry you made them, there would always be at least one person (ahem) that was always on your side. It was strangely comforting.

"So you just expect me to bandage you up like I did last time, like nothing happened." It wasn't really a question, and I sat perfectly still, not even nodding because I knew he wasn't asking for an answer. Cade was fuming, not that I could blame him. He just needed to blow off a little steam, and I could wait for that. I had sent him away from the bar, and to him, it probably didn't matter that I had done it for his own good. It wouldn't matter that I had done it so that I could find out more about my mom without having to worry about him. It wasn't because I didn't trust him; that couldn't be further from the truth, because I trusted him more than I trusted anyone else in this forsaken little town; I trusted his brother only because, as much of a smart aleck as he was, he also genuinely seemed like he was a good person, even if it was buried deep. Way deep. Still, none of those things would matter to Cade right now. As far as he was concerned, I had sent him away when he was trying to help me.

Part of me wanted to point out that I could have asked Liam to patch me up, because he was just as capable of doing it as Cade was, but I didn't want to. For one thing, I trusted Cade more than I trusted Liam, and I didn't want to hurt his feelings any more than I already had. I knew that was why he was so upset, because I had hurt his feelings when I had sent him away, and it would be a while before he was in the right frame of mind to listen to any reasons that I might have for having done that. I wasn't going to hurt him any more than I had to, which meant that I had to be patient with him, even if it was pushing my buttons. I hunched my shoulders and did my best to look penitent, which wasn't hard considering that every move-ment hurt. I might have thought that I was pretty much healed before I went back to the bar for the umpteenth time, but getting manhandled had rapidly undone all the healing and then some. And it had gotten me precisely nowhere in finding my mom, although I did at least know who had framed me for the robbery. No idea why, other than the general knowledge that my father was an opportunistic jerk, but progress was progress.

"I'm sorry. My father isn't exactly the kind of person that I want to introduce my friends to, and I needed him to think that I was weak so that he would feel safe telling me about my mom." My cheeks were a bit flushed, and that was probably just because of the fact that I had admitted they were my friends; it certainly wasn't because of what I had said about my father, because that wasn't exactly difficult to tell, especially since I had no doubt that Cade had come straight back here and vented to his brother. I didn't have very many friends, as evidenced by the fact that not one of the kids that I had gone to school with had reached out to me in the weeks since I had vanished to make sure that I was still alive and hadn't been abducted by aliens. These two were the closest things that I had to family, which was pretty sad considering that I had known the other kids since we were in diapers and I had known these two for only a few days.

Cade sighed, finally seeming to lose steam in his

tirade. "Did you find anything out about your mom?" The two of them seemed just as invested in helping me find my mom as I was interested in finding her, which was part of the reason that I had panicked so much when he had showed up at the bar. I didn't want either of them to get hurt on my account, especially since neither of them had anything to do with Mom, helping me find her, or the blackmail ring that my father had dragged me into. This wasn't their problem, as much as I appreciated the help, and I was scared to death that they would get hurt just as badly as I had. If not worse.

I shook my head and their faces fell. We were all understandably upset about it, but I hadn't given up hope just yet. "I don't think she was ever here. I think it's some sort of spell that leaves a trail here for someone to follow. But on the plus side, I did figure out who is behind my recent little crime spree." I smiled crookedly as I quickly explained about Lou and what my father had said. On the one hand, I wanted to tell them so that they knew exactly how crazy my father was, even if Cade hadn't already figured that out on his own. On the other hand, if that was what one of my parents was like, then I wouldn't have blamed them if they had wanted to ditch me and avoid trying to find Mom all together. No matter how many times I assured them that Mom was nothing like my father, it wouldn't matter if they were determined not to listen. It was dangerous for them to be involved. If Lou could do this to me, then she could do it to anyone. Just like me, I doubted that anyone would stand up for the boys, and no one would miss us if something happened to us.

Liam stepped away and came back a moment later with a piece of paper and a puzzled expression. I too had heard the knock at the door of the garage, but I hadn't moved, figuring that it was someone that was here to get a part or speak to the owner of the shop, neither of which we could help them with. Ernest hadn't been around much, to the point that I didn't even know whether or not he knew that I was staying here. I didn't want to get kicked out of here, but I also wouldn't have blamed him if he had found out that all of us were shacking up here. The boys had permission. The wanted felon and the magical guard dog, not so much.

Whatever assumption that I had made about the contents of the letter were dashed when Liam slid his finger under the seal and slit it open. I could see now that it had been addressed to me, but he didn't seem the slightest bit bothered by the fact that he had just opened something that could have been private. And why would he? Maybe that was a perk of not caring about anyone else, because it didn't matter what anyone else did, because he didn't care about us or anything resembling common decency. Either he was seriously nosy, or he thought he was going to take a look at something for some reason that I didn't know.

Who knew? Whatever the reason, I still wasn't in the mood to argue with him about it. Besides, there were very few people that knew I was here, so this was gonna be good.

"What does it say?"

He looked up at me. His skin was a bit ashy, which concerned me. He wasn't like Cade, who was more free with his emotions; if Liam was acting this way, then it had to be bad.

"Lou wants to meet you in the middle of the desert. I think it's a trap."

CHAPTER EIGHT

~

"It's a trap! You know it is."

I sighed and pinched the bridge of my nose. Maybe if I squeezed hard enough, I could somehow knock myself and escape from the pointless argument that the boys insisted on having with me. Unlikely, but not impossible.

"Yes, it is almost certainly a trap. But I don't have much of a choice. As long as everyone thinks that I'm a bank robber, they hold all the cards. If I do what they want, then maybe they'll let me go." I knew that it was extremely unlikely, but it wasn't impossible. I still didn't know what exactly was going on with the whole blackmail thing, other than a nagging sensation that I wasn't the only one that had been on the receiving end of such illustrious treatment from my father and his hench girl.

Finally, the boys gave up arguing with me. Cade stalked out to take a walk and Liam disappeared into the next room, which left me to prepare to meet Lou. Boo whined softly, sitting up as I climbed onto my bike. I shook my head at her. I knew she wanted to come with me, but right now was not a good time.

"Not this time, pretty girl." I rode away, equally as unhappy to be leaving her as I was to be meeting Lou at all. But I didn't have a choice.

"What do you want?"

Lou rolled her eyes, but just because she was out here in the middle of nowhere with me, that didn't mean that I was going to treat her any differently than I had at the bar. I still wanted to thank her for the slap with one of my own, but I figured that if she was going to be out here with me, probably without my father's permission, then it had to be something good.

"Your boys are in danger."

I squinted at her. I had no idea why she would tell me this. There was no good reason for her to warn me that something was going to happen to the boys, since it would only be to her benefit, but here she was. Plus, how would she know? I wouldn't put her past doing something to them, but then why would she warn me? None of it made any sense. "Why are you telling me this?"

She shrugged. "Because just like your father, I think that you are a very powerful witch, and I like to be friends with other witches. I don't think that we would still be friends if I didn't warn you that something was going to happen to them. Consider this a friendship bracelet." She grinned crookedly. Clearly there was something a little skewed if she considered this to be a friendship bracelet, but I did appreciate it if what she was telling me was true. As if on cue, my phone rang, and I stepped away to answer it. I didn't know the number and normally that meant that I wouldn't have answered it, but I was feeling a little twitchy right about now. I wanted to know what was going on, even if that meant answering the strange number that popped up on my phone. I stood with my back to Lou as I answered the phone, still keeping a wary eye on her over my shoulder as I spoke.

"Hello?"

I hadn't actually met Ernest yet, but somehow, I knew it was his voice on the other end. I counted myself lucky that I could understand him at all, considering how fast he was talking. I unconsciously made a "slow down" gesture before I realized that he couldn't see me. I glanced back at Lou, not surprised at what Ernest was saying. He said that he had come back to the garage just in time to see the boys being taken, so he had followed the car they had been shoved into; I was duly impressed by his bravery, but somehow I didn't think that someone his age would be able to get the boys back alone. Once I finally managed to get him to slow down enough to explain to me where it was, I promised that I was coming to help him and quickly hung up. Eyes narrowed, I turned to face Lou.

"Somehow I don't think that you warning me about the boys being taken is a coincidence. Actually, I think you might have had something to do with it." The timing was too similar for it to be a coincidence. "If I find out that you have something to do with this, I'm going to make you sorry." We both had magic, and it rose at the threat, but I wasn't scared of her. I didn't have very many friends, but if the ones that I did have had taught me anything, it was that I was very protective of the few I did have. If they got hurt and she had something to do with it, I was going to make her pay, and the same went for my father. They both might have already had it coming because they had framed me for the robbery, but I was surprised to find that I was more upset about the boys than I was about myself. They could mess with me, but messing with my friends was out of bounds.

She swept a low, mocking bow as I climbed onto my bike and jammed my helmet into place. If she said anything else, I didn't hear it, because I was already speeding back into town to help Ernest with the boys. Even if she had said something, I didn't think I cared very much.

Good news and bad news. The good news was that Ernest was waiting for me, and the even better news was that Boo was waiting as well, sitting pretty in the bed of his ancient, powder blue truck. I had no idea if he had brought her or if she had decided to come on her own, since I wouldn't have been surprised by either option. She had, after all, wanted to come with me, and she was probably feeling the same way that I was now: if she had been with me, I would have felt much safer, but if she had been with the boys, then she might have been able to protect them. Instead, she had been stuck at the garage and hadn't been able to help any of us. And right now, I wasn't going to ask, because I had bigger things to worry about.

"I take it that you're Ernest." I reached out to shake his hand. He looked like the grunge version of Santa, complete with a scraggly gray beard and dirt under his nails. His grip was firm, and if he had any reservations about the fact that I had been staying in his garage this whole time, then he hadn't mentioned it yet. Either he didn't know, or he didn't care, and right now was not the right time to find out. Still, I wanted to thank him later, when this was all over, and if he didn't know about me staying there, then I would deal with that. That was what Mom would have wanted me to do.

"So, young lady. Do you have a plan for how you're going to get our boys back?" I hooked onto the fact that he said "our", which somehow made my chest feel all warm and squishy. They might have been his definitely, but I wouldn't have considered them mine until I tried to reject the idea and it made my heart hurt. True, I had already admitted that they were my friends, but knowing that they were in danger made me panic more than I had expected.

I motioned at Boo. I had no idea if she would be able to track them down or not, but I had the utmost faith in her. Besides, she had a better chance than I did. At least we had a basic idea of where they were, rather than trying to search the whole world; I was again thankful that Ernest had had the presence of mind to follow the boys, although it did make me wonder why he hadn't tried to intervene. Maybe the situation hadn't been right, maybe he hadn't been able to get there in time, or maybe he was just afraid. Whatever the reason, I didn't want to embarrass him by asking. Besides, it didn't matter. Maybe Lou had lured me away into the desert because she had somehow been part of the plot to take the boys, or maybe she had genuinely wanted to warn me about the boys and had just been too late. Either way, I hadn't been there to save them either. I had no room to talk.

"She's going to find them. We know that they're here, and she knows their scents, so she's going to track them down." He looked down at Boo, clearly impressed, and I hoped that I hadn't oversold her skills too much. I had never tried to ask anything like this of her, and even though I had the utmost faith in her, I could only hope that faith would be enough. I leaned down to gently kiss the top of her head, then leaned on the gate to open it. If there was anyone in here, they had probably been part of taking the boys, and I was pretty sure that we were going to have a problem anyway; therefore, I didn't care if I made noise. I was fairly sure that Boo could have hopped the fence, and I could have too, but walking through the gate was the more logical solution, not to mention the fact that I highly doubted that Ernest would be able to jump the fence. There was no need to show off.

Boo had her nose to the ground as soon as she entered the junkyard, weaving through the old cars, tractors, refrigerators, bed springs, and who knew what else that was hidden in the piles of mud around here; belatedly I wondered if she had her tetanus shot, because the last thing that I needed was for her to get lockjaw because of all this. It was almost entirely silent as of right now, and I didn't trust that at all. I wanted to talk to Ernest, to thank him both for letting me stay in his garage and also for calling me when he had followed the boys here, but I didn't want to distract Boo from what she was doing. I hadn't given her anything that belonged to the boys to smell, probably because I didn't have anything, so I could only hope that she was following the right scent. I was going to be very upset if she ended up leading us to the nearest pizza joint. Not that I could blame her, but still. She was going to make us look bad.

It was a good thing that we were all being quiet. If we hadn't been, then we never would have heard the pounding. Boo barked and took off like a rocket, her long legs launching her forward as she leapt onto an old car. I hadn't thought that she was that heavy, but apparently she was, because her weight buckled the lid of the trunk inward, and she hopped down and trotted back to me with a satisfied woof. The trunk lid creaked open and we all stared, unsure of what was going to be coming out of there; true, it was probably the boys, but given the streak of luck that I'd had lately, I wouldn't have been surprised if it had been some kind of eldritch horror. If it was, then it was Boo's problem, because I was so drained the best thing I could do was throw a few punches.

Nope, thankfully. It was the boys, Liam shoving out first and falling rather ungracefully onto the ground, followed by Cade. Boo went to check them out, giving them a few cursory sniffs, and I leaned down to check on them. They were a little bruised, or perhaps scuffed was a better description, but it didn't look like they were any worse for wear. I didn't know what to ask them, because clearly they weren't okay, having just been kidnapped, but not asking them seemed cold.

"So. Are you okay?" As expected, they both unleashed a look of absolute loathing in my general direction, then rolled their eyes. I could tell that they weren't actually angry with me, just a little irritated and probably shaken up, so I didn't take it personally. Feeling bad that there was a good chance this had only happened because of me, I explained about Lou calling me to warn me about them being taken, and they shared my sentiments that she must have had something to do with it. I had no idea why they had been taken, other than to remind me that I wasn't in control of the situation, something that I was unfortunately very well aware of. If it was a threat, then whoever had been in charge hadn't been very good at their job; there hadn't even been a ransom demand, and there was no one around to make sure that they didn't escape. The whole thing felt wrong, like it was unorganized and had been thrown together, but people didn't just decide to go out and kidnap people. Then again, given the people that I had met in this town so far, maybe they did.

That left the five of us to find our way back to our various vehicles. Boo and I led the way, mostly because I was thinking, but also because Ernest seemed to want to have a conversation with the boys, and I didn't want to bother him. I didn't know what they were talking about, and it was probably better that way. It was none of my business.

I crossed my arms, looking at Boo. Her lean body was sprawled over the top of my bike, and her tall ears pricked as she looked at me. She straightened up, sitting firmly on the back of my bike. "What do you think you're doing, dog?" It didn't look like she had done any damage to my bike, which I was glad of, but that didn't mean that it would be safe for her to ride on the back. I vaguely remembered seeing pictures and videos of dogs riding on the back of motorcycles, but those had been little dogs, small enough to fit in a basket on the back. They had not been massive Dobermans who were half as tall as me.

"So where am I going to sit?" Cade asked. Boo was still sitting in front of the bike, and she showed her teeth to Cade as he approached. The seat that I'd had made was still firmly in place, but even though I could have folded it up and put it into the saddlebags on my bike, Boo didn't look like she was willing to give up her spot; I hid a smile as I thought of what it would be like to watch Cade fight Boo for the spot. I wasn't particularly in a mood to chat, and where I was going, having a Doberman with me was a whole lot better than a mechanic. If it came down to it, it was probably better that he didn't ride with me.

"Take that up with the dog." I grinned, looking at Ernest out of the corner of my eye. He was still around, which meant that Cade would still be able to ride with him. Boo hopped into her seat, growling at Cade. He hesitated, but Ernest gripped him by the back of the neck and pushed him toward the truck. It was eerily similar to what had happened to me several times in the last few days, but the spirit of the gesture was very different. He glanced back at me, as if he could sense that something wasn't quite right with me, but I forced a smile and waved at him. I was about to do something dangerous, and I didn't want him to be around for it. No doubt he and Ernest would be furious when they figured out that I wasn't, not to mention that I had intentionally not told them that I was going to do something stupid. On the one hand, I had been doing stupid things since long before I had met them, but I still felt weirdly connected to them, like I owed them something. Against my better judgement and despite all that had already happened between us, I was pretty sure that we were becoming friends. That was as dangerous for them as it was for me, something that I didn't want to admit. I could almost sense that there was danger, but I had no idea when or how it would happen. Boo reluctantly climbed back into the bed of the truck and we all headed back to the garage. Ernest hadn't said a word when we arrived, which told me that he had already known that I was staying here and didn't care, but it still felt strange.

I couldn't shake the sense that something bad was going to happen. I sat outside, staring up at the stars as I hugged my arms around myself and tried not to flip out every time I heard something. I had expected that Boo would be sitting with me, but she was inside, probably taking her job as guard dog seriously after what had happened to the boys today, not that I could blame her. There was a soft click and my head jerked up, startling me so badly that I fell backward, instinctively throwing my hand out to strike with magic. Just like before, the magic went through the creature in front of me, but that was the least of my problems; hands grabbed me and a hood descended over my head, plunging me into darkness.

I struck out as hard as I could, but caught a whiff of my father's magic, pinning my arms to my sides and preventing me from screaming, at least out loud. I sat as still as I could, verging between panicking and then, once I had calmed a little, trying to recognize anything that was going on around me. If there was anyone or anything that I could recognize for later, then I was going to get back at them. For now, all I could do was wait.

EIGHT

~

Sticking my nose into other people's business was what I did best, but considering the situation that I had gotten myself into this time, I was starting to consider becoming a hermit. Somehow my dad had found out that I had taken Boo, and the bikers had come to grab me in the night. They were going to make an example of me, but of course, Lou had something else up her sleeve.

"Stand still," Lou muttered. "And be quiet." I could feel the gun pressed against my back, and I did as she said; it was less a conscious thought and more of my brain telling me that if she was capable of making everyone think that I was a criminal, she was more than capable of shooting me in the back without a second thought. I wasn't sure why she had told me to stand still, since it didn't make much sense. For one thing, if she had done it just because she didn't want me to move around or she was irritated by me messing around, then she wouldn't have whispered it so that only I could hear it; she would have said it so that everyone could hear how tough she was being. For another, if she was actually going to shoot me, then she wouldn't have told me to be quiet at all; she would have just shot me. I could feel the stares of the rest of the gang boring holes in my back, and I hesitated. I wasn't sure what the orders were that she had been given, especially now that Dad was gone; I couldn't see him, and I highly doubted that he would have left of his own volition. Of course, I was fairly certain that he might have told her to shoot me even if it had been him, but at least then it wouldn't have been an execution in front of everyone. No matter who the order had come from, it was all about to end badly.

"Keep moving," Lou snarled, giving me a shove toward the back room. I threw a glare over my shoulder, but I could see something in her eyes that wasn't quite what I would have expected if she were going to murder me right here. She didn't look like a murderer, but I didn't know her, and I didn't trust her. But I might have to if I wanted to get out of this alive.

"Don't worry about it," one of them called. "Just do it right here. We don't mind cleaning up a little blood."

I swallowed hard. That was the bad thing about having hardwood floors in a bar; if there was blood or alcohol on the floor, a mop and some cleaning solution would solve the problem rather quickly. I hated how easily all traces of me could be erased, and no one would notice if I disappeared. Other than Ernest and the brothers, and I didn't want them to get hurt if they tried to come after me. If they tried to find me, or avenge me, it would be too dangerous. It occurred to me that I should have left a note to the effect, but it wouldn't have done any good. I hadn't exactly intended to be here, but I should have made some sort of plan of what would happen if I got in over my head. Of course, I hadn't thought that it would matter that much, nor that it was worth the effort. Given the fact that Lou was about to shoot me in the back, I maybe should have rethought that position, but it was too late now.

Lou sighed. Her eyes rolled, but to me it looked like a show that she was putting on for the onlookers. If she was going to actually kill me, it was going to be hard to do it right here. If she wasn't going to, which was what I was hoping for, it was going to be hard for her to be that off with all these people watching.

"Fine." I heard a click as the gun cocked, and I closed my eyes. If she was going to shoot me, there was nothing I could do about it. I could feel my magic coiling, preparing to take the impact of the bullet, but there was no guarantee that it would be able to stop the bullet, especially from this close to my body.

The gun cracked, and searing pain exploded along my side. I fell forward, folding to my knees. My natural instinct was to put my hands out to catch myself, but that wasn't something that a dead body would do. Instead, I tried to tuck my chin against my shoulder to minimize the damage, but I was still jarring to land face first on the hard floor, my cheekbone striking the hard wood so viciously that I was sure I would have been seeing stars if not for the fact that my eyes were already closed. I could already feel the bruise forming on my cheekbone, but I held as still as I could, trying not to even breathe. Mom had always called it playing possum when I faked being asleep as a child; that was pretty much what I was doing right now, except I was pretending to be dead, and there was even more at stake than before. There was a scuff of boots on the floor, a whistle of air, and a jagged stab of pain as a foot struck me in the ribs, right where the bullets had made their home. I wasn't sure whether they had embedded themselves beneath my skin or whether they were simply scrapes, and it wasn't like I could roll over and check, considering the fact that I was supposed to be dead. The pain was savage as the foot struck again, and it took everything I had to stay still and pretend that I was dead. I instinctively retreated into my magic, wrapping it around me like a comforting blanket. It didn't change the fact that I was in pain, but it did dull it enough that I could stay still. I heard everyone leave the bar, the door slamming closed as they chuckled and spoke, but I waited a few more minutes, my ears straining, before I tried to move. I would have liked to have said that it was because I was making sure that everyone was gone, and that was partially true, but I was more worried about the fact that I just really didn't want to get up.

Mom hadn't raised a quitter, even if I did want to curl up in a ball and cry; even that would require me to get out from under this blanket of magic, which meant that I needed to move. I pushed myself off the floor, trying to focus more on the push-up than the fact that it felt like my rib cage was trying to swear. Or maybe that was just my brain. It was the first time I had been shot, and it reminded me of what Mom had always told me: gunshot wounds and magic didn't mix. She had never given much explanation as to why, and I had never asked her, probably because I hadn't thought that I would have much occasion to worry about it. No one expected to get shot, and I certainly didn't, especially not this soon in my life; Mom had always been very against me following in her footsteps, but she had finally given up and agreed to take me on a few trips here and there. I didn't know what I wanted to be when I grew up, but I had known enough about my dad to know that I was not going to follow in his footsteps, down the criminal path. Dodging a few truancy officers here and there was not the same as committing actual crimes, which was part of the reason that Lou's crimes as me had hurt so much. I knew that she had only been doing what she was told, but that didn't make it any easier to see my face on a wanted poster, nor was that going to do any favors for whatever career I chose in the future, unless that happened to be actually becoming the criminal that everyone seemed to believe I was destined to be. Even worse, no one would believe me if I told them that I wasn't responsible for the things that everyone said I had done. I could just imagine a meeting with the college recruiter now. Yes, that looks like me, but it was actually a witch who can shapeshift into anyone, and she was using that power to blackmail people. But don't worry, she was doing that at the behest of my father, who alternates between being a crime lord and the leader of a motorcycle gang, and both he and my mom left me. Yes, I did drop out of school for a few months, but that was only to find my mom. Even in my head, the scenario did not end up working out in my favor. I managed to get out to my bike and ride slowly back to the garage, barely keeping it together for long enough to stagger inside.

"You know, for someone as big and bad as you, you sure do get hurt a lot. Almost like a damsel in distress." That was Liam, and I stared at him with my mouth open. He wasn't wrong, but I was still insulted. Up until

I had come to this town, I had been perfectly capable of handling myself, but since Mom had disappeared, my head wasn't in the game. She was one of the best bounty hunters out there, and I knew that she was hoping that I wouldn't follow in her footsteps, but that hadn't stopped her from taking me on a few gigs with her. I had always done fine on them, but since she had left me, I had gotten beat up, shot, and lured into a trap that I should have seen coming a mile away, although in my defense, I had never had enough friends to worry about them being used against me. Of course, at this particular second, I wasn't sure that I would call them friends. More like nuisances. I couldn't believe that they would talk crap to me like that, and I would have liked to have pointed out that I regretted saving them. That wasn't true, because I could never have left them to an uncertain fate, but that didn't make it any easier to deal with their attitude.

I yanked my shirt down, fighting a wince as it yanked on the bandage on my side. Should have known better than to yank it around like that, although, to be fair, I didn't normally have to worry about that when I had an attitude because I didn't normally have a bandage on my stomach. Just like Mom had always told me, the gunshot wounds didn't seem to be healing as fast as some of the other ones, and I could tell that they were going to leave some pretty gnarly scars on my ribcage. Then again, considering the crowd of people that wanted my head on a platter, a crowd that was growing bigger every second, I just counted myself lucky to be among the living. Besides, scars were cool sometimes. At the very least it would be an interesting story to tell somewhere down the line.

I hopped off the table, crowding Cade enough that he backed off as I leveled a glare at his brother. Cade wasn't the one that I was mad at, but he was the one that happened to be in my space. "You two are the ones who got yourselves kidnapped. I'm no damsel in distress." I huffed. "I have places to be." Not really, since this was pretty much the only place in the city that I could be where everyone didn't think I was either dead or a bank robber. I was itching for a fight with someone, anyone. At this point, Liam was the best option, and the most likely to get punched. If we ended up cooped up here for any length of time, then this might get ugly.

Cade shook his head firmly, put a hand on my shoulder, and pushed me back down on a table. Part of me was tempted not to let him move me, but that was petty; Cade hadn't done anything but help me, and there was no reason that I should punish him for his brother being an insensitive butt. Besides, the only reason that I was so mad at Liam was that he was right.

"You, sit down. Liam, shut up. You don't need to antagonize her, especially not right now." There was a thin line of lime green magic that crawled between fingers, and I sighed as the pain eased somewhat. I hadn't known that Cade was a healer, and it made me wonder why he hadn't used it before. Not that I was angry about it, but I was a little miffed that he hadn't thought to share that with me before. As if he could sense my irritation, the magic receded, and he sat next to me. "My magic only works sometimes, and with injuries that won't interfere with other magic. Gunshot wounds don't draw on your magic to heal, so I can work on healing it." I could see how pale he was, and it was clearly taking its toll on him. I leaned toward him, then changed my mind and slid off the table, standing in front of him. I was no further away from him than I had been when I had intentionally been crowding him, and he didn't move back, just like Liam hadn't when I had challenged him in the bar. I looked Cade in the eyes, making sure that he was well aware of what I was saying.

"I appreciate it, but you look like death warmed over. I'm a tough girl, and I'm not going to let you hurt yourself because of me. It'll heal when it heals." He still looked like he was about to fall asleep on his feet, and I glanced back at Liam, who was watching us both. There were only two cots in the garage, and we had been taking turns sleeping so that we had room, or sleeping on any other surface. Sometimes it was a fight to see who would get which cot, especially since there was nowhere else to sleep in the garage, not even a couch or a chair, but right now there was no doubt that Cade needed it more than either of us. I shot a glare at Liam, daring him to say anything otherwise, but he met my glare calmly and slid under Cade's other arm, helping me help him onto one of the cots.

"I think you should get some rest," Liam said, offering a rakish grin. He had taken up residence on the other cot, and lifted the blanket invitingly. I glared at him, wishing suddenly that Mom had taught me to hurt people with my magic in more ways than she had. There was no possibility that I was going to give him the satisfaction of crawling into bed with him, even if there was nothing going to happen, for several reasons. First and most important, there was no way that I was going to make out with him. Secondly, Ernest had been an absolutely phenomenal, if somewhat absent house-mate thus far, but I still didn't think that he would be okay with us sleeping together in his garage. And besides, I could do something even better.

Cade still looked like he was half dead, but I could tell he was awake, because his eyes flickered open when I stopped next to his cot and carefully kicked off my boots. I didn't have many clothes to wear other than the leather jacket that I had and various pairs of jeans and dark tee shirts, which also meant that there was nothing really more comfortable that I could change into. The best I could do was take my belt off and drop it next to my boots, then step over the cot. "Cade, can I join you?"

Liam snorted, and I met his challenging glare. Clearly he hadn't considered that I would do something like this, which only made it more entertaining for me. I didn't want to make Cade uncomfortable, which was the reason that I had asked. Besides, the cots weren't really meant for two people, and I didn't want him to have trouble sleeping because of me. I was proving a point, but even asking has proven it; if Cade didn't want to share the cot with me, then I was more than happy to sleep on my bike or on a table somewhere.

While I might have thought that Cade was the calmer, less rakish of the two brothers, he did still have the temperament to want to push his brother's buttons. He didn't even blink before he lifted the blanket and I crawled onto the cot with him, although I left as much space as the cot would allow. I didn't want to turn toward him, because that was awkward, but it would be even more awkward if I turned away from him. As if he could sense the dilemma, he rolled on his side as well, so that the two of us could sleep back to back. Boo had been on the floor for most of the day, near me. I had expected that she might choose to sleep with Liam, since he had the only space in a cot that a dog of her size might fit into, but no. Instead, she squeezed onto the cot between Cade and I, her head resting between our shoulders. It was uncomfortable, but weirdly comforting to be able to feel her heartbeat against my back. I closed my eyes and tried to rest, but I highly doubted that sleep was going to come anytime soon.

And I was right. I was still awake when the door creaked open, and my eyes shot open. Anyone that belonged here would know how to avoid making that much noise, which meant that someone was here that shouldn't have been.

"Cade, wake up," I hissed, shoving his shoulder. It wasn't safe for any of us to be here, even if they were only here for me. Every roughneck in town knew that they were with me, which meant it was no longer safe for them. Unfortunately, there was nowhere for the three of us to go on the back of my motorcycle; I was a good rider, but three people on one motorcycle was not going to work. They just weren't made for that. On top of that, there was an even bigger problem: Cade was still unconscious, and I was trying hard not to judge him for how long it had knocked him out to use his powers. I had never heard of anything like his abilities, nor were they anything like mine, so I had no room to judge him for how he reacted to using them. At least, that's what I told myself, but it was hard to remind myself of that when I had to figure out how to get Sleeping Beauty out of here when the baddies showed up.

Liam hustled back in, panting from running from the window where he had been standing to the back room where Cade and I were hidden. I was shocked that he hadn't taken off, but then again, that might have been because we were between him and the back door; he couldn't have snuck out without us if he had wanted to. Or maybe that was just me being mean, but at this point, I couldn't have said.

"You carry him, and I'll try to distract them," Liam whispered.

"I'm strong, but not deadlift-your-unconscious-brother strong." I had never tried to carry anyone like that before, so I didn't know that for sure, but I did have a pretty good idea that it wasn't going to work. I slid under Cade's arm again, pulling him off the cot. Liam went under the other arm, but he craned his neck. I knew what had caught his attention. My tattoo, which was a phrase in Latin, wrapping around my upper arm. It was almost a match for the one that Mom had in the same spot, although that was just one of her many tattoos. She had always been very cool about whatever I wanted to do with myself, as long as I understood the implications of it. Most of what I had done had consisted of dyeing my hair when I was younger, although I did have piercings in the cartilage of both ears. The tattoo was the only one that I had, just like the one that Mom had in the same place, although her phrase was different than mine. My favorite of hers was hard to choose, although I had to say that it might be either the feathered snake wrapping around her calf or the one above her heart, which was my footprints as a baby with my birthdate and how much I had weighed when I was born. It was weird to see that, mostly because I didn't want all of my personal info out there like that. True, it was on my mother's chest and I hoped that there weren't too many people that would be seeing that, but it wasn't my place to judge. If there were, so be it. I didn't think that he was judging me, but at this point, I didn't care if he was.

"Nice tat," he whispered, and I rolled my eyes. Between the two of us we were able to get to the back of the shop, to where all of the bikes and vehicles were hidden. While right now it may have been used more for fixing motorcycles, there were still pits in the floor, just below the lifts where the cars would have been placed. There were no stairs that I could see to get down into them, but there were doors that would cover them, which meant that they were the best hiding spot that I could see at the moment. I could still hear our unwanted visitors rattling around outside, which only made me more nervous.

I jumped down into the pit. Good news: it wasn't that far, and I didn't break an ankle jumping in like that. Bad news: I hadn't really thought out how we were going to get Cade down here in the pit. Apparently neither had Liam, because his solution was to crouch down and basically toss his brother at me. I was strong, but I hadn't been strong enough to carry him, and I definitely hadn't expected to catch all his weight coming from above like an unconscious avenging angel. I staggered backward, trying not to fall over or drop him on the ground; I ended up folding in a not very graceful way, with him all but in my lap. Liam stood over us to pull the doors closed, plunging us into almost complete darkness.

We all waited in tense silence as the sounds of the shop being ransacked continued above. Cade being down for the count was probably a blessing in disguise, especially since he likely wouldn't have shut up otherwise. Even after we were sure that the men were gone, we waited. Just to be sure.

NINE

~

"So do we know who those guys were?"

It was a rather redundant question, since I doubted the boys knew if I didn't, but I felt like it was a question that was still worth asking. It was a pretty decent guess to think that our visitors had been the bikers that we had all irritated, even though I would freely admit that it was a charge led by me, but we didn't know that for sure.

Once our unwelcome visitors had decided to leave, albeit with much swearing and rattling of everything still left in the room, we had finally come out. Getting Cade out of the pit was an adventure in and of itself, but that was the hard part; once we were done getting him up, we carried him to his cot and laid him back out, but neither Liam nor I seemed inclined to head back to the other cot. I was so wound that I felt like I could climb up a ten story building with sheer force of will, which meant that I needed to chill out.

I was curled up on the table with my legs crossed, partially because there weren't that many places to sit and partially because this way I could see where everyone was; it was just the three of us in here and one of us was unconscious, but it was still my instinct, and I couldn't help it. Unfortunately, it also meant that I was sitting on a flat surface with no back, which was not the most secure arrangement if someone, say, decided to push me off the back. Just as an example.

"Someone's coming," Liam hissed. Before I even had a chance to move, he took care of the problem for me; one hard shove and I tumbled backward, falling off the table and rolling backward. If I hadn't had such good reflexes I might have cracked my head open, but I managed to turn my rather ungainly fall into a roll so that I didn't hurt myself too badly, although obviously landing on a concrete floor didn't feel great. I poked my head up to snarl at him, but heels clicked on the concrete, and I disappeared from sight again. I was still going to yell at him later, but until I figured out who was here, it was time to hit pause on that.

"So. You three are ridiculous. Boy wonder used a handful of magic to do absolutely nothing on a bullet wound, and he's now knocked out. And I kill her so that she's got a way out of town. Instead you idiots decide to break into the lair of the people who want you dead."

I squinted above the table, startled by what I was seeing. The only person that would have "killed" me was Lou, but it didn't seem like she was the one talking. The woman standing in front of us was an older woman, wearing short heels. She looked like a secretary, or the type of person who started an argument in a grocery store about expired coupons. In other words, she couldn't seem any less like Lou than she did, but that didn't mean anything when someone could change what they looked like. I would have to take the chance that it was her before I revealed myself, not that our situation left me much choice. If it was Lou, then she already knew that I was here, and if she had wanted me dead, she could easily have done it already. That didn't make it any easier to straighten up, and Boo growled at the woman standing in front of her, which was a sentiment that I wholeheartedly agreed with.

"Back off, pooch," the woman warned, returning to Lou's form in a matter of seconds. Boo whined again, which was something else that I agreed with. It was extremely disconcerting to see her switch forms, although it was better now that she wasn't wearing my face; that was something that I didn't think I could ever get over. Still, it was comforting to know that I didn't have to worry about Boo mistaking us; even wearing my face, she still wanted nothing to do with Lou and stuck close to my side.

Lou rolled her eyes at us. I hadn't expected that she would be in the greatest of moods, but that still didn't explain what she was doing here. "What do you want?"

"I have another tip for you, since you did so well with the last one." She looked at the boys. Liam was glaring at her, and I could tell by the way he had his body angled that he was instinctively trying to protect his brother. He hadn't looked at me, not once, but he did seem to understand that I would do whatever I had to to protect Cade, if it came down to it. Yes, we did owe her for warning us about the boys, but since she had shot me, I considered us even. "Another aspect of your dear father's business plan is kidnapping, along with blackmail. You're the first one from out of town that we've blackmailed, but he chose another target for the kidnapping, the daughter of a local businessman."

"So let me get this straight. The gang is forcing you to blackmail people, and their latest scheme is kidnapping someone's little girl?" Unfortunately, I could see it, and it made sense. It was almost exactly the same thing as they had done with me. By committing a robbery with my face, Lou had made sure that I did what they wanted or they would make sure that a whole lot more people with badges, other than the truancy officers, were chasing me. It didn't matter that it had been a set up, probably a fake bank with actors and no real crime;

all that mattered was that someone with my face was on video robbing a bank and seen walking out of the front doors with a lot of money. Given how terrified everyone in this town was of the Pit Vipers, I wouldn't doubt that they could gather up a whole host of witnesses that would say they had seen me commit the crime. I'd already gotten the warning, loud and clear: stay out of their business, die, or spend the rest of my life in prison. I didn't particularly like any of the options.

Liam rolled his eyes, although he did lean forward. "Why should we believe you? Given what you've done so far, I think that the jury is still pretty far out on whether or not we can trust you?" I felt a little bit of warmth in my chest. Lou hadn't technically done anything to the boys, and yet both of them were very firmly against her, acting as if what she had done to me was as unforgivable as if she had done it to them. I would have been the first to admit that I didn't have many friends, so having gained two, three if you counted Ernest, in the past few days was a bit of a shock. It was strange to think that the only reason that they disliked Lou was because she had tried to hurt me, but I did still appreciate the thought. Cade was starting to wake up and have even managed to sit up, which was a good sign, but I wasn't sure just how caught up he was with the situation right now.

Lou gritted her teeth. "I honestly don't care if you

believe me. I came back here to make sure that she was healing okay after I shot her, but the rest of it I can deal with myself. I'll figure something out."

"No, you won't," I said firmly. The three of them looked at me, and I straightened up, despite the twinge of pain from the bullet wound in my side. The bullet wound was healing fairly nicely, even without magic to heal it, and I was going stir crazy having to stay in this garage. That didn't mean that I wasn't grateful to the boys for letting me stay here, because I was, but it was still a bit boring to have to stick around here and hide from the gang, who seemed to have eyes everywhere. Sooner or later they were going to have to figure out that I wasn't dead yet, because I wasn't about to give up on my mom and hide out here for who knew how long.

"Whoa!" Liam said firmly, holding out his hands. "We need to talk about this." He grabbed my arm and Cade's, pulling us off to the side as he tossed a suspicious glare over his shoulder at Lou. She looked totally bored with the whole conversation, but I didn't doubt that she was listening to every word that we said. Not that I could blame her, considering the fact that she was in danger every second that she spent with us, not to mention that they would kill her if they ever found out that she hadn't done the same to me. It would have been far easier for her to just kill me and be done with it, although I was glad that she had decided not to; I didn't understand why she had decided not to. I just couldn't wrap my head around it.

Cade, thankfully, was waking up rather quickly; I was glad that he was finally getting with the program, but just because there was another person to argue with did not mean that I was just going to give up. There was no way that I was going to leave a little girl in the hands of anyone that might mean her harm, including her father. The reasons to trust and the reasons not to trust Lou were pretty neatly balanced right now, which meant that there was no way I was going to take that chance.

"We need to talk about this," Liam repeated insistently. I rolled my eyes, but I was secretly glad that he seemed to care. Still, there was nothing to talk about. There was no way that I was going to let a little girl stay in the hands of the madmen-and women- that had tried to kill me. I had already done enough stupid things this trip to last me a lifetime, but I didn't think this was stupid. Reckless? Absolutely. Potentially fatal? Probably. Stupid? Never.

"There's nothing to talk about. We have to help."

"This isn't our job. Call the police and let them deal with things." I could tell how much it made him suffer to advocate talking to the police, probably just as much as it did me, but it wasn't going to change my mind. By the time the police were able to authenticate the tip from such an admittedly dubious source, it would be too late. We could already have been there and back.

"We're not as heartless as you make us out to be. Can you really see the picture of a little girl and decide to just leave her high and dry?" I gestured to the muted TV behind him, which had been playing the story of the little girl on repeat for hours. Her photo was on there, a picture of her in a pink dress with a unicorn headband. I didn't consider myself to be a hardened criminal, nor was I the kindest person in the world, but even I couldn't look at her face and leave her in such a bind. I was almost totally certain that Cade would be on my side, and Liam might be if I could play my cards right, despite his protests. Still, that didn't mean that I was going to make any assumptions. Honestly, it didn't really matter to me. I wasn't going to leave that little girl. Either they could help me, or I would do it myself. I was stubborn enough that I didn't care which.

"This is the worst idea that we've ever had. We don't even have good masks," Liam grumbled. I snickered, pulling my mask over my head to let it settle around my neck. It wasn't so much a mask as it was a scarf or a gator (was that what it was called?). It rested around my neck when I wasn't wearing it; when I was, I pulled it up over my nose and mouth so that on;y my eyes and forehead were visible. No matter what it was called, it still covered my face just fine, better than the old ski mask that Cade had dug up. Liam had a bandana around his neck like an ascot; his was just a precaution, since I was hoping that he wasn't going to be anywhere near us. His job was to keep watch while we were inside getting the little, so if he ended up inside with us, either he wasn't doing his job correctly or we had some bigger problems to deal with. Knowing him, there was a good chance that it might be both.

"Speak for yourself. I'm as well dressed as any self respecting bank robber." I fluffed my hair over my collar for a second, play primping for a moment because I was going to pull my hair back in a ponytail. Even though that's not what we were doing, I was hoping that it would help Liam loosen up. I had expected it to be Cade who protested against our little escapade, since he was the only one out of us that seemed to have any good sense, but he remained quiet. Liam was the one who hated the idea, probably because it meant putting his own skin on the line. Still, both of them stayed with me, and they didn't seem inclined to go anywhere else. We all took up our positions as we snuck inside. Not for the first time, I was regretting that Boo hadn't been able to come with us, but we couldn't guarantee her safety, and I didn't want anything to happen to her. Once we were inside, it didn't take long to find the little girl. Again, it would have been easier with Boo, but we young humans managed it just the same.

I pulled the mask down from my face so that the little girl could see that I wasn't a "bad guy", although at this point anyone on a motorcycle with a leather jacket might have fit that bill, at least in her mind. My hair was pulled back in a tight ponytail, as was Liam's; the hope was that if anyone saw us, they would think we were the same person, since we weren't supposed to be in the same place at the same time. He was the lookout, since he had the loudest voice, and we all knew that he could talk trash with the best of them. The best we could hope for was that he figured out if someone was coming and gave us plenty of time to get out before he ever had to use his silver tongue to get out of a dicey situation.

I pulled my knife out of the pocket of my leather jacket, and the little girl, Charlotte, stared at it with a mixture of horror and fear. "I'm going to use this to cut the ropes so we can get you out of here, okay? I don't want to hurt you. I just want to get you out of here before the bad guys come back." I reached behind her, sawing at the ropes as carefully as I could. It was a sharp knife, as sharp as I could keep it, but that didn't make it any easier to cut a squirming little girl around the ropes that were too tight on her slender wrists. Other than some bruises and general disarray, especially around where they had tied her up on her wrists and ankles, she seemed relatively unharmed. Still, if she didn't stop moving, then she was going to end up with a few cuts on her wrists because I wasn't able to not cut her with her squirming like a worm on a hook.

"All right, sweetheart. I'm going to need you to get on the big bike with him. This is Cade. You'll be safe with him, I promise." It was a promise that I wasn't sure I could make, but it was something that she needed to hear. Besides, she was as safe as I could make her, and Cade would do anything that he could to make sure that she was okay. We were all in danger here, but only the boys and I were used to constantly being in danger; a little girl like Charlotte who had grown up with a family that loved and sheltered her would never have been in a situation like that. Mom had always kept me safe, but I would be the first to admit that I had been in some dicey situations because of her, but I wasn't angry with her about it. It had made me even more sure of myself, and it had made me sure that I could handle almost anything. Now that might not have been true, but I had done a pretty good job convincing myself.

"Wait a second. What are you going to do?" Cade hissed. Liam still hadn't come in, but I would have been shocked if he hadn't taken off to save his own skin. Not that I would have blamed him; it just would have been nice to have a little bit of warning if he was going to take off, but his missing bike kind of told the story for itself. I buried my fingers in the cloth of my mask, ready to pull it up, but I figured that I at least owed Cade an explanation of what I was going to do, especially if it was as stupid as I thought it was. He had no offensive magic, not like I did. If we got caught in here, the Pit Vipers would kill us, no question in my mind. Just as importantly and in an adjacent problem category was the fact that if they killed us, poor Charlotte went back to being a hostage, and I wasn't about to let that happen. We had promised that we would get her back, and I kept my promises.

"You take her. I'm going to ride out the other set of doors and see if I can get some of them to follow me." I figured that if they heard our bikes rev, then it wouldn't be long before they were on their own. If I could get them to follow me instead of realizing that there were two of us, then it would give Cade time to get away. I hoped.

Cade grabbed my arm and I fought the urge to sigh and/or roll my eyes. I should have known better than to think that he would let me get away with doing something so stupid, or at least not without a fight. I stared at him, leaning toward him as he tugged on my arm; I didn't have to move, but I was going to humor him, especially since Charlotte was around and I was pretty sure that it would scare her to see her two would-be rescuers get into a shouting match before we ever got out of the building with our heads intact. Both of us were already on our bikes, with Charlotte between us. I could easily have reached down and pulled her onto my bike, but that was leaving too much up to chance. It would be painting a target on our backs, and I couldn't do that to Cade or Charlotte. I didn't like being the bait any more than the next person did, but it was better than all of us ending up dead, right here and right now. I trusted that Cade would be able to keep her safe, and I had faith that I could get out of this. Blind faith, maybe, but faith nonetheless.

Cade stared into my eyes for a moment more and for a second I thought he was going to kiss me. My brain froze, locked onto the black rings in his eyes and the dark bruise on his cheekbone that he had gotten helping me. I wasn't sure whether I was for or against the idea of him kissing me, but I did know that right now wasn't the right time for that sort of thing. Still, I held perfectly still as I waited for him to make his next move. Finally he sighed and his eyes flicked up, freeing me from his gaze.

"I don't like this, but I can't talk you out of it, can I?"

I shook my head and grinned, trying to make light of the situation. He was absolutely right, and I was glad that he was able to realize that. "No. But you know me so well." It was only partially a joke. Yes, we had only known each other for a few days, but we had been through a lot in that short span of time. I had always been sort of a lone wolf, and that had only gotten worse after Mom had disappeared and left me on my own to deal with everything. True, she had probably thought that she was doing the best that she could, making sure that the bills were paid so that I didn't have to, but she should have known better than to think that I would just sit at home and wonder what had happened to her. She hadn't raised a quitter, and she certainly hadn't raised me to leave her when there was a chance that she needed me, now more than ever. Even if I couldn't find her, it wouldn't be for lack of trying.

I took a deep breath, pulling the mask down so that I could put my helmet on. I rarely wore my helmet, certainly not as often as I should have, but I wasn't taking a chance that I got hurt pulling a stunt like this. There was a pretty decent chance that I was going to take a spill, if I didn't get shot, stabbed, or otherwise injured, but I knew one thing for sure. If something did happen, I was not going to let Cade even try to heal me, not after I had seen what it had done to him before. It was kind of counterproductive that he would knock himself out trying to heal me, so I wasn't going to let him. Of course, it was almost certain that I was going to get hurt, but I was still going to do my best not to. Just, you know, for the sake of common sense.

I took one last look at Cade and Charlotte, who was now on the front of his bike, cradled in his arms. He wasn't wearing his helmet, and I wished that we'd had the good sense to bring one for Charlotte at least. With our hard heads, we could probably manage to survive something that most other people couldn't, but Charlotte was a child. It wasn't like any of us had a helmet that would fit her, but if we had been thinking, we should have tracked one down for her to wear; I would have felt like a real idiot if we had saved her from a biker gang and then have her get hurt while we were making our escape, because no doubt this was going to be a rough ride. Even with me doing my best to be a distraction, I wasn't sure that I could get all of the bikers to follow me, but I could only hope that Cade would be able to deal with the rest on his own. I was already risking life and limb to lead them away; there was literally nothing more that I could do.

I kicked my bike to life. At almost exactly the same time Cade did the same, and I flashed a grin at him despite the seriousness of the situation, impressed again by how smart he was. By starting his bike at the same time I had, he was making sure that they only heard one bike, which would make it easier to convince them that there was only one of us leaving. As long as I could get them to follow me, then they wouldn't know that Charlotte was gone until it was too late. That was the only reason that I was glad that there were two doors back here; while it did mean that we didn't have enough people to cover all the entrances, it also meant that I could go out one door, Cade could go out the other, and no one would ever know that there hadn't been only one of us until it was too late.

"Ready?" I asked. Charlotte was buried as deep as she could be without actually entering Cade's chest, so at least I didn't have to worry about her falling off, no matter how fast they went. Cade looked somewhat ill with anxiety, which was exactly how I felt, but one of us had to keep it together if we were going to get out of this. Actually, both of us had to keep it together, me so that I could lead the baddies away from the ones I cared about, and Cade because he had to be the savior I knew he could be. I knew that he could do this without me, even if he didn't seem as sure about that as I was.

Now the hard part. I rolled my bike to the front, while Cade went to the back door and opened it to make sure that there was no one back there, because if there was, then this whole thing was over before it could even begin. He looked back and shook his head, which clearly meant that there was no one back there, despite the fact that I could see lights in the front of the building that also happened to be the direction that I needed to go. It was now or never.

We both rode off, and I concentrated on staying just far enough ahead of the other motorcycles that they would think they had only one quarry to chase. I kept the count in my head, and only once I had made sure that the brothers were long gone did I find a way to slip away from them, slipping through an alley and circling back around before they had a chance to catch up with me. I rode for a few more minutes, making sure that no one was following me, then headed back to the garage, only to walk into an argument.

At first I thought that the argument was something

about Charlotte, only to realize that she was nowhere to be found; that wasn't overly alarming to me, since the poor thing was probably exhausted and probably needed some time to rest and freshen up. No, the argument seemed to be with Ernest, and it was only after I had heard a few snatches of it that I realized what the argument was about. This, then, must have been the reason that Liam had bailed in the middle of our dangerous mission without telling anyone. I had known that it had to be important, but I had never imagined that it would be something as diabolical as this.

I stared at the sign on the garage, my brain struggling to comprehend what was happening here. I had known that something was strange with the cursed parts that Lou had mentioned, just as a reference to the blackmail that she had been a part of, but I had never even considered that this little shop where I had been staying for the last few days would be involved in something as nefarious as that. It made no sense, and yet when I considered the evidence, not to mention the very ashamed older man in front of me, it made all the sense in the world.

"Really, Ernest?" This was his garage and I was just the girl who had been sleeping on one of the cots here for the past few days, and yet he had the grace to look ashamed when I glanced at him.

All three of them looked at me and flushed. I rolled

my eyes, not at all surprised that they hadn't intended for me to find out about this little escapade. As far as Ernest was probably concerned, I had no right to know anything about the business that he ran here, and the boys probably didn't want to scare me away. Maybe that was why I wasn't surprised when Lou showed up to drag me off to the side, because she seemed to show up like a bad penny, every time there was a sketchy situation happening. Still, I could either deal with her or try to jump into the argument with the guys, and I knew that she would be the lesser of two evils, at least this time around, so I let her pull me into another room, and we made ourselves comfortable. The guys could figure out their troubles on their own, without me stepping in to interfere.

"So why me?" I asked. We hadn't been able to get a hold of Charlotte's parents, probably since it was the middle of the night, so she was curled up against my chest, holding me like I was a teddy bear. I didn't blame her. It was scary enough for us to be the ones to go in after her, but she was a little girl, taken from her parents and held by big, scary men for no reason that she knew; I couldn't imagine how scared she was, and I felt awful that she'd had to go through it. She was rather heavy and the hammock that we'd rigged up for me to sleep in wasn't comfortable for one person, let alone two, but I didn't have the heart to wake her up and make her sleep somewhere else. Besides, where would she sleep? I had either slept on my bike or with Cade since I had gotten here, and the hammock was only a recent addition; I wasn't about to dump the poor thing on the floor, so it looked like she got to sleep with me tonight, provided that the hammock didn't break and make it so that both of us ended up on the ground. Her head was buried in my chest so tightly that I was worried she couldn't breathe properly, but every time I tried to scoot back to give her some room, she just moved with me. Her thick golden curls shifted as she breathed, and she had her fingers hooked in my belt loops, like she was afraid that I was going to leave her in her sleep. She may have ridden with Cade, but apparently she had decided to attach herself to me. I smiled a bit, but there was still the matter of Lou, who had shown up for who knew what reason. Yes, she had told us about Charlotte in the first place, but I wasn't dumb enough to think that she had done it out of the goodness of her heart.

Lou glanced up. She looked like herself for once, not someone else's face, or at least was wearing the face that I thought was hers. There wasn't really any way to know, since she was a shapeshifter, but it hurt my brain trying to figure out which face was actually hers, so I was just going to work off the assumption that this one was hers and go from there; after all, this was the face that I had first seen her with, so it was the best guess I could come up with. Otherwise, I was going to drive myself crazy every time I saw someone new, or even someone that I had already met, trying to figure out if they were actually someone new or if it was just Lou messing around with us. I already had enough stress in my life without adding extreme paranoia to the list.

"What do you mean, why you?" I gestured at her, then back at myself. As far as I knew, I was a nobody, and yet the Pit Vipers had taken enough interest in me to make her create a fake crime that they could blackmail me with. I hadn't even known what they were called until the boys and I had started asking some questions, but the name seemed oddly appropriate. I was pretty sure that I wasn't important enough to bother with, especially once I saw the other rackets that they had their sticky fingers in. Robbery, blackmail, kidnapping, protection rackets. Beating me up might have been deserved, since I had gone in there like an overconfident idiot, but framing me for a crime that I didn't commit and then having me "killed" when I refused to cooperate? I didn't get why it mattered.

Lou looked at me like I was an idiot, which unfortunately was a look that I was getting all too used to. I did freely admit that the stunt I had pulled while we were saving Charlotte had been stupid, but considering that it was just the latest in a blooming career of stupid and dangerous stunts, I didn't get why anyone was surprised. I had walked into a biker bar and picked a fight, broken into their storage unit after they had given me the beating of my life, and made them angry enough that they tried to have me killed; it shouldn't have surprised anyone that I was willing and able to continue adding stupid to my newly impressive roster.

"Because you marched into the bar like you owned the place. Anyone that can be as big of a thorn in their side as you were is someone that they want on their side."

That made sense. They probably weren't used to anyone acting like I had, especially if everyone in this town was as afraid of them as they seemed. I was probably the first one in a long time that had given them a run for their money, and even I could tell that I would have been useful to them if I had done as I was told. I had magic, not to mention being able to ride a motorcycle and fight, although that last one probably hadn't been on great display the last time we fought, since it had been like twenty against one. Every occasion since then hadn't gone much better, but apparently I had made an impression. Lou seemed inclined to leave after our conversation, so I followed her out and went back in to check on the boys. Apparently Ernest had decided that we should take Charlotte to the police station, so it was just the three of us here. Well, four of us if you counted Boo. Of course, the boys had taken it upon themselves to find out more about me, and that included finding out more about me and my relationship to my new dog, as if that was the most exciting thing to be found here.

"What, do you hate dogs or something?" Liam challenged; I could tell that he didn't, since he was desperately trying to lure Boo toward him with a piece of the meat from his sandwich. Sprawled at my feet, she lifted her head and took a deep sniff, but refused to leave my side; I felt a sense of smug satisfaction. I stroked her back gently, my fingers trailing along her short, silky fur. It wasn't that I hated dogs; I didn't have enough experience to hate them. We'd always lived a fast life, which made sense since my mom was always chasing bounties and my dad had been out of the picture for most of my life. Mom had always told me that anything worth doing is worth doing well, and the same went for caring for an animal. We always had to be ready to pick up and get out of town at a moment's notice, and we couldn't take the chance that a pet would be left behind, because neither of us would have been able to live with ourselves if something had happened to a beloved pet. Besides, it wouldn't be fair to a dog to not be able to give it enough attention. I had always wanted a dog, since Mom had taught me to value loyalty above all else, but it had just never been in the cards. Now I had a dog who had quite literally taken a chunk out of me, all the way down to the magic in my blood, and I couldn't imagine not bringing her with me. Still, if I didn't find Mom soon, then I was going to have to move on, and I didn't know if it was going to be in the cards to bring her along. With the boys here, at least I knew that they would take care of her for me, but that still didn't make it any easier to think about giving her up.

I shook my head, still gently stroking Boo's back. "No, I don't hate dogs. I just grew up without any pets, so I'm still getting used to her." I didn't want to leave her here, but I also wasn't sure that it would be safe for her to come with me. She was a big dog and could no doubt take care of herself, something I knew from the teeth marks that were still clearly visible on my body, but I didn't want her to get hurt because of me. Then again, if what I had read was true, I wasn't sure that I could get rid of her if I had wanted to. And why would I want to, since she was probably my familiar, something that I was just now starting to wrap my head around.

Mom was a good witch, but she had limited knowledge on certain things, and as hard as she had tried to teach me everything she knew, there were still some gaps in my knowledge. There were also things that she had left me notes on that I hadn't paid much attention to, probably because I hadn't thought it would be of much use to me. That category included familiars. I hadn't been allowed to have any pets as a child, so why would I want a familiar? Besides, having a familiar was kind of like being married, except you could never get rid of each other without going out of your way to break the magical bond between the two of you. Still, I had been looking through her books, the notes that she had left me in my journal, and I had found a mention that told me that maybe Boo was as stuck with me as I was with her.

There were two ways to create a familiar. One way was to create an animal entirely from magic, which was a dangerous and complicated process, one that I hadn't even bothered to try because I knew that I would mess it up somehow. What if I messed it up? I couldn't be trusted with something as simple as tracking down my missing mother, although it had turned out to be anything but simple; still, it made me think that trying to give life to a creature entirely from my magic, magic that I could barely use for anything but hurting people, made me think that it wasn't a good idea. Knowing my luck, I would accidentally create some kind of giant lobster or something like that. That, and I had never really needed a familiar. The same reason that I had never had a pet applied here: I had to be ready to leave at a moment's notice, and this little adventure with the boys had taught me that that was even more important now. However, there was something else that I hadn't thought of, something else that I hadn't known before but had found in Mom's notes. Familiars of both kinds could sort of fold themselves in space and time, which meant that they could basically teleport all on their own. Only the most powerful ones could take their masters, or mistresses, with them, but they could jump if they wanted to. It made it easier to think of what could happen, and what I could do if I didn't have to worry about her. If she could come with me whenever and wherever I took off to, without me having to worry that she would be stuck somewhere and starve, it would make things easier on the both of us. More importantly, it meant I wouldn't be lonely anymore. How could I, when she refused to leave my side for more than a few minutes at a time? Still, it was a relief to know that I would never be without company.

Oh, and the second way is for an existing animal, one who has been exposed to magic, to connect directly to the source of magic in their new master or mistress. I hadn't been able to figure out what exactly that meant at first, but now I thought that it was probably good enough that she had bit me, especially since I knew that she had come into contact with my magic when she had. It was possible that she had gotten enough of my magic to form a magical link between us, although I couldn't have said that for sure until now. And again, it was just a theory, one that I had no way to prove or disprove until I found a more experienced witch than myself to ask. Who knew when that would happen?

I stood up, and Boo glanced up when she felt my fingers leave her back, her eyes curious. Both of the boys glanced at me as well, especially as I crouched next to Boo, smiling playfully at her. She sat up and I gently cradled her head in my hands, looking into her liquid brown eyes. I had never had a familiar before, so I had no idea how I was supposed to communicate to her what I wanted her to do. It was more a request than anything, simply to see whether or not she could do what I thought she could, but she wouldn't care about that. Still, it made it harder for me to figure out how to articulate what I wanted from her. I didn't think that she could read my thoughts, or at least I hoped she couldn't. It was one thing to have a dog read my thoughts and entirely another to have another human being poking around in there, but I would still prefer to have it entirely to myself. I was pretty sure that I was safe in that department, but just to make sure, I thought, as hard as I could: *Steak.* I figured if there was any word that was going to get her attention, then that was it, but she didn't react in the slightest, just kept watching me with her loving, intelligent eyes, which meant that I was safe.

Almost immediately I felt bad. Here I was, having accidentally made her a familiar against her will, or at least not when that was what she had been intended for, and I was acting like it was some kind of terrible burden that I had been saddled with. She had already proven on more than one occasion that she was as loyal as anyone else, if not more so, so I couldn't believe that I had been so unkind in my thoughts about her. She was a good dog, even if she couldn't read my thoughts, and we would still be able to figure out what we needed to do to communicate. I still wanted to know whether or not she was capable of teleporting like I thought she was, but I had no idea how to make her understand what I wanted from her. It wasn't something that came up in everyday conversation, and neither of the boys were going to be much help, especially since neither of them had familiars, and I wasn't even sure that Liam had magic. I knew Cade did, but he didn't have a familiar. For a moment I envisioned what it might be, whatever manner of creature would fit him best, but now was not the time. I was easily distracted at the best of times, but I knew myself well enough to know that I was just trying to avoid doing what needed to be done. Both Boo and I deserved to know what she could do, and I wasn't going to put it off any longer. There was nothing to be gained and a lot to be lost.

I whispered to Boo, trying to explain what I wanted from her. I still wasn't so sure that she wasn't smarter than me, but I didn't know if I had the words to explain what I wanted, so it was up in the air what she could figure out for herself. Then I stepped away, ignoring the boys and their questioning glances, so that I could head outside and hide somewhere on the grounds of the garage. I chose behind a high wall of tires, where I could still see the entrance of the garage but where no one else could see me. I hadn't explained to the boys what I was planning, mostly because I didn't want either Boo or I to be embarrassed if it didn't work out like I had thought it would. I wasn't sure that she could even be embarrassed, because I wasn't exactly in the know on how canine brains worked, but I didn't want to take that chance. Then I sent her out, her long legs pumping as she sprinted away from me. I had told her to teleport as soon as she got to the pile of tires outside, and now I just had to wait to see if it would work. Maybe it would or maybe it wouldn't, with plenty of reasons that it could go either way. She could not know what I meant by teleporting, because it was a difficult concept to explain to even a human. Or maybe she did know what I meant but just couldn't do it. Or...the list of possibilities went on and on.

I should have known better than to think that it wouldn't work; she was too smart for that. Once she reached the tires, there was a shimmer, and she disappeared. A few seconds later she was next to me, burying her wet nose in my shoulder and the crook of my neck. I giggled and curled up, keeling over on my side as she continued to lick me, clearly taking my movement as a sign of weakness and wasting no opportunity to press her advantage. I pushed on her chest in a feeble attempt to shove her away, but I didn't want to hurt her, and she was too solid of a dog to be deterred by something as small as that. Finally she gave one last huge slurp, from my chin to my eyebrows, and hopped off me with a satisfied woof of pride.

I sat up, rubbing my face and glaring at her as I tried

to wipe all the spit off. There was no way that I was going to be able to get rid of all this saliva, or at least not anytime soon. The boys were staring at us with their mouths hanging open, which meant that they had seen what she had done and were now trying to connect the dots between what they had seen and what actually made sense. Easier said than done, at least when it came to this. There were far too many things about this situation that didn't make any sense, and unfortunately, answers weren't likely to be forthcoming, especially if they didn't know about familiars. I had a feeling that they might not, but that was an assumption, and you know what they say about assuming.

I would have liked to have said that I only wanted to know about whether or not Boo could teleport just because I was curious about her talents or what familiars could do, but that would have been a total lie. I had a bad plan that I was turning over and over in my head, trying to think if there was any better way of going about it that I hadn't thought of yet. Thus far I hadn't been able to come up with anything, and the best I could offer was that a dog who could teleport was going to be a real help for a plan like this. After all, what fun was it to do something stupid without a friend?

~

"I hate this town," I muttered under my breath, more to myself than anyone else; it wasn't that there was no one around, because unfortunately there was; it was more that I didn't want to admit that I had been wrong. It had been my own bad decision to try to take back my mother's bike, or even to get anywhere near it, and now I had gotten myself into trouble again. I grabbed Boo and tried to boost her up, then instinctively flinched as a shot went off. Hopping a fence would be far easier would have been far easier if someone wasn't shooting at us, but Boo had that locked down. Or, at least, that was what I gathered when she grabbed my arm in her teeth and the world spun again.

I sat up, glancing around for the other rednecks who happened to have been shooting at us just a second ago. Unfortunately, getting shot at was becoming a pretty regular occurrence of late, and the only thing that made this time different was the fact that none of the boys, nor Lou, had been with me. The only backup that I had brought was Boo, who was sprawled on the ground, her tongue lolling as she panted. She looked exhausted, but more than that, she looked proud of herself, and I knew why: because she had teleported. Not only had she teleported, she had managed to take me with her, and even if we had ended up in the middle of nowhere, it was still a pretty good job, especially since this was the first time that she had tried to teleport under pressure. Sure, she had managed to take me with her during our trial runs in the garage, but that didn't mean that I had assumed that she would be able to do the same thing in a dangerous situation. As it turned out, she had been able to, like the magnificent creature that she was. I had just been planning on hopping the fence when they started shooting at us, mostly because she hadn't seemed inclined to teleport and I hadn't been able to get myself together enough to ask her, but she had taken care of things on her own.

I gently gripped her collar and pulled her toward me, hugging her tight. I couldn't believe that I had treated her the way I had at the beginning, and I was especially ashamed of the fact that I had somehow been ashamed to have her as my familiar. True, I don't think that either of us had meant for the connection to be made, but she had already proven that she was more than capable of holding her own, not to mention that she was as loyal and loving as anyone else that I had encountered in my life, if not more so. I was lucky to have her, and there was nothing that was going to make me feel any other way about her.

"You're such a good girl," I whispered in her ear, gently running my fingers over her body to make sure that she was okay, that she hadn't been injured during the jump. I didn't exactly know what the protocol was for whether or not she could accidentally get shot while we were doing whatever teleporting actually was, and I wasn't going to take that chance with her. Once I was finished checking her over, I gave myself a quick pat down, just to make sure that I wasn't hurt, either. I didn't feel any pain, but with as much adrenaline as was running through my veins, I wouldn't have been surprised if there was a gaping wound somewhere that I wouldn't even have noticed.

She may have had only the stub of a tail, but that wasn't going to stop her from letting me know just how happy she really was; her whole back half wagged, and she gave one ecstatic lick on my face before something caught her attention and she whipped free of my grip, snarling as she whirled to face whatever the threat was. I was impressed by how quickly she could go from absolutely loving to about to maul someone in the span of a few seconds, but I needn't have been; I was capable of the same thing, especially if I was hungry. I crawled onto my hands and knees, flexing my fingers in the sand to call my magic and ground myself. Things had been a bit squirrelly with my magic of late, but I wasn't above throwing sand in someone's eyes if it came down to it. I may have been a martial artist, but rules were for tournaments; if it came down to playing dirty and saving my own skin, or Boo's, then I was more than happy to do all the mean things that would never have been allowed to do in a tournament. Mom had always taught me that the winner of a street fight was the one that got to go home that night, even if there was a stop at the hospital on the way. If that meant throwing sand and magic, or either of those things, then I was perfectly happy to do that.

The boys panted to a stop, both of them dropping their dirt bikes on the ground with a crash as they sprinted toward us. Boo had already stopped growling and had returned to my side, nudging me gently as she sniffed me all over; no doubt she was checking me over as thoroughly as I had her, now that she was sure that our new visitors posed no threat to us. Other than being exhausted, I didn't think either of us had anything more than a few bumps and bruises, which was a small miracle considering the danger that we had been in just a few minutes before. I had no idea why Boo had chosen this particular location to bring us, not that it mattered. It was just that I had always thought that familiars needed to know a certain location before they could teleport there, and I had my doubts that she had ever been given this much room to roam in her life, especially considering that she had been on a chain when I had found her. Why, then, had she chosen this of all places to bring the two of us? She deserved as much room to run as I could give her, and I resolved to make sure that she had the home she deserved. She was a good dog, and she deserved to be treated like the queen she was.

"How did you find us?" I asked. We were walking back to the dirt bikes flopped in the sand, slowly in my case because I was still feeling a little shaken up from our rough landing. Boo was slower than usual as well, but she was still more than capable of trotting circles around all of us with something that was either smugness or glee. Liam flushed, staring at the ground. For a moment I thought he wouldn't answer me, but Cade nudged him, then lengthened his strides so that he was walking ahead of us. I raised my eyebrows, wondering what could make him give his brother so much space to tell me. It was either very juicy or very bad. Honestly, with these two, who knew?

"I can find people. The more I care about you, the more I can sense you. That's how we found you."

Startled, I glanced at him. We were miles out of town and Boo and I were the only ones that were anywhere near here; somehow I doubted that Boo was the one he sensed, which meant that he must have had a very good sense of me to be able to sense me this far. I glanced at him out of the corner of my eye, surprised that he was admitting that he cared about me. It wasn't as if he was declaring his undying love for me, but the fact that he had even admitted this much meant a lot to me. After all, we had only known each other a few days, so it must have meant something. I could have teased him about it, but I wasn't going to reward the trust and affection he had shown me by doing him wrong like that. Instead, I slung an arm around his shoulders and pulled him close, not saying a word as I hugged him. The flush on his cheeks darkened, and he started at Boo like she was about to speak. If she did, I was really going to jump out of my skin, and that was the last thing that I needed today. Of course, we couldn't have gotten lucky enough to get out of here without getting ourselves in trouble, since the three of us seemed to be trouble magnets.

Liam's head jerked up, and he gave me a shove toward the bushes. "Hide!"

I didn't hesitate. Maybe that made me a coward, or maybe it meant that I was becoming more confident in the boys, because when I heard the dirt bikes coming and saw the brothers stand shoulder to shoulder, I didn't immediately feel like I needed to protect them. I needed to trust them, and I was trying to make that happen. Plus, it had already been a rough day, and I was more than willing to take a dive if it meant that someone else could be in danger for once.

"You two stay where you are. But if Renegade doesn't get out here in the next two minutes, I'm going to shoot one of you." I could hear my father's voice, and Boo growled softly at my feet. I didn't think he would shoot one of the boys, but I couldn't take that chance. I did the best that I could to bury my magic; every time he was near me, it felt like he was draining me dry, and I was smart enough to realize that it wasn't just stress.

"Could you point that a little higher?" Liam asked. He sounded almost as amused as normal, but the request did make me roll my eyes. Even with my magic pushed down I could still sense that there was more than one person here, and the request made curious who was pointing the gun at him but more importantly, where were they pointing it?

I did some quick math in my head, but no matter how I twisted the situation in my head, there was never an end to this situation that didn't end with at least one of us getting shot. My father was a lot of things, but he wasn't the sort of person that would make a threat that he wasn't more than willing to carry out. I wasn't sure how long it had been since the ultimatum had been made, how much of the two minutes had passed, not that it really mattered; it wouldn't do me any good to wait, and the longer I did wait, the better of a chance there was that I was going to end up getting someone shot. Besides, two minutes didn't seem like a long time until someone's life was on the line, and then things got very messy, just like they were right now. There was nothing to be gained by waiting, and everything to be lost.

"Wait!" I straightened up, raising my hands up by my head. It was less to show that I didn't have any weapons and more to show that I wasn't using magic; if these people were with my dad, then they would know that I had magic, and it wouldn't do me any good to pretend that I didn't. It might irritate them further, which was the last thing that I wanted; I was more than willing to be a smart aleck if I had been the only one here, but I wasn't, and it wasn't the boys' problem that I had a smart mouth when someone tried to tell me what to do.

The girl holding the gun gestured with it for me to come forward, and I instinctively tensed when she pointed it at me. It wasn't Lou, not that that would have been more comforting for me, considering that she had already shot me once. Actually, since she had shot me once and hadn't killed me, I might have preferred that it had been her; I would have had a better chance of living that way. "Fine. I'm right here." Boo was walking with me, growling softly, and I was trying to edge forward enough to get next to the boys. I had a plan, but there were so many things that could go wrong they made my head spin. I wasn't sure that Boo had enough oomph left in her to make another jump, let alone dragging the three of us back into town with her. I had no idea how we were going to all hold onto her, nor how I was going to get the boys to get the message without warning our enemies about the same thing. They might have had an idea of what she was capable of doing, but they hadn't seen it happen with their own eyes, at least not yet. Still, with a gun pointed at us and nothing to lose, now was as good of a time as any.

"Boo, now." I lunged forward to grab her, counting on the fact that the boys would reach for me. It was a natural instinct for them, or at least that was what I was guessing, and that was the reason I was willing to take the chance. I just had enough time to realize that I was right before the world twisted again.

This time, the landing was much rougher. It wasn't Boo's fault; all magic got a little squirrely when we were tired, and even if it had been something that I was willing to talk to the dog about, she had still been the one to save all of our bacon, which meant that I was going to keep my mouth shut. We all slammed onto the hard floor of the shop, and I groaned. I didn't know who was on the top, and I didn't know who was on the bottom, but I dang sure knew who was in the middle. Me.

I kicked myself free of the pile, not even bothering to be gentle; I didn't have the energy for that right now. I flopped onto my back as the boys disentangled themselves, bickering, and Boo flopped onto my stomach. She was rather heavy and made it hard to breathe, but considering what she had done, there was no way that I was going to begrudge her a little bit of time to cuddle. I kissed her head gently. The boys crawled toward us and bestowed kisses as well.

"Good girl." I had no reason to be jealous, which Cade's glance told me that he was worried about, and every reason to be proud of her. Still, there were other things on my mind.

"Where was she pointing it?" I asked Liam suddenly. It was very much not important, nor was it pertinent to the danger that we had just gotten out of or the danger that we were currently in, but I just couldn't help but wonder where she had been pointing the gun that would make even cocky Liam nervous enough to say something. Typical teenage angst, I guess.

"What?"

"The gun. Earlier, when you said something about pointing it higher, where was she pointing it at?" I could feel the beginnings of a flush creeping up my cheeks, but it was too late to back out now. Besides, even if I was a little embarrassed at where my mind was going when I imagined what could have prompted him to say that, I was still too stubborn to let it go. I had asked the question, and now I wanted the answer.

Liam gave me a strange look from the corner of his eye. I would have expected that he would say something snarky, but he seemed to be all snarked out for the day; I couldn't exactly blame him. I was exhausted too, and poor Boo looked like she was about to keel over from exhaustion. Even Cade looked tired, although his was probably more from stress than it was from anything else, since he hadn't had an occasion to use his powers today. As far as I was concerned, he never needed to use his powers for me again. For one thing, I was a pretty tough girl, and I had grown up knowing that if I was dumb enough to get myself into a situation where I got hurt, then that was my own fault, and I was going to have to deal with the consequences of that choice; nothing had changed. That, and a power that left him so zonked out that passed out immediately afterwards wasn't much use to us. Liam might not feel the same way, but I didn't really care what he thought most of the time.

"At my knee. Where did you think she was pointing it?"

I wasn't going to give him the satisfaction of an answer, but it wasn't hard to imagine. Let him think what he wanted. I wasn't going to shrug or nod or do anything else, so I just stared straight forward, my fingers brushing Boo's back as we walked. Liam's smirk didn't disappear, which only made it harder for me not to smack him. Instead, I ignored him as much as I could.

It was a quiet night back at the garage. Even though Ernest was part of the ring that was peddling cursed parts, I couldn't bring myself to say anything to him about it, not after he had been kind enough to let me stay here for so long without asking for anything in return. Besides, until we were sure that everyone was taken care of, I couldn't ask him to put both his life and his livelihood in danger by standing up against the people that had dragged him into all of this in the first place. That didn't make staying here any easier, especially when I thought about Mom, and how this had all started.

I sighed, gently stroking Boo's head. There was no way that I could leave her behind now, even if I did find Mom. I just couldn't do it. She was my familiar, and I could feel the ache in my chest when she was away from me. I had been scared that since I had no experience with pets, I wouldn't be good enough for her, but she didn't seem to mind. Her head was sprawled across my lap, her ears tipped up as her liquid brown eyes studied me. The look in her eyes was absolute adoration, and I could feel the warmth in my chest as I looked at her. I didn't deserve her. Come what may, she was coming with me. After all, a witch is stronger with a familiar, and I would need all the strength that I could get if I was going to beat my father and get all of us out of this mess.

ELEVEN

~

Now came the time to deal with my father which, in this case, meant that I had to go and blackmail him. Ironic how things turn out, isn't it? That's the funny thing about karma: whether it's your teenage daughter or the universe itself, someone will always be there to make sure that you get your just desserts.

"So you lied to me. Just like you always do." I should have known better than to think that my father could be trusted, even when it was with something as deceptively simple as where my mother was. She would never have wanted him to know where she was, which was probably why I had been able to convince myself that he might know where she was; if there was one thing that my dad lived for, it was spiting people. She might not have wanted him to know about it, but I had been smart enough to figure it all out, and now I was at a dead end. I could practically feel Mom's pride from here, that I found out what she wanted me to, except she hadn't wanted me to. She had come here to take care of the ring herself, and the fact that I had been the one to break it up did not bode well for where she was or what might have happened to her. It had now been weeks since I had heard from her, and I knew that if she had been able to, then she would have contacted me already. The fact that she hadn't concerned me, but right now my focus was my father. He had lied to me about what he knew about my mother, not to mention the things he had done, although I supposed that no one wanted to admit that they had committed a whole host of crimes. He wasn't ashamed of it, because that would require some sense of morality, but he wasn't willing to give me anything to hold over his head. That meant weakness, and he couldn't allow that.

He scoffed. "I'm hurt. But to be honest, I wasn't looking for her. Imagine my surprise when my long lost daughter shows up right in my backyard."

I rolled my eyes. Of course he would only care about Mom because it brought him closer to me. And don't let that make it sound like he cared about me, because that wasn't the case at all. He only decided to care when it served him, and I knew that better than most. I should have known better than to think that he actually cared about me because I was his own flesh and blood. Plus, point of fact, I had never been "lost". I just hadn't chosen to associate with him once he had left us, mostly because I had never felt any kind of urge to track him down. If he wanted to leave, then let him stay gone.

"Here's the bad news, Dad. Ernest isn't the only one in this town that you've been blackmailing into selling your cursed parts. So here's what's going to happen." There was a sort of high in being able to tell him what to do, but I warned myself not to get too attached to that feeling. My father was not the sort of person who could be taken lightly, especially since he had so many people on his side. He didn't like being told what to do any more than I did, but that didn't mean that we were the same. He would hurt someone if it came down to it, something that I could never bring myself to do. "You're going to disappear, and all of the blackmail is going to disappear with you. If you don't, then everyone that you have blackmailed will step forward to testify."

His eyes narrowed as he studied me, clearly trying to decide if I was lying to him or not. I was; I didn't think that Ernest, or anyone else for that matter, would be willing to step forward and take on my father and his thugs. That wasn't the point. The point of this was that I wasn't going to let my father walk all over everyone in order to get what he wanted. Mom might not have wanted me to come here, but I was going to take care of this while I was here. Unfortunately, he was the one that had taught me to lie, and I might have inherited a little of that deceitfulness from him. He might have thought I was lying, but he wasn't willing to chance it. Without another word, he spun on his heel and stalked away, leaving me to huff a sigh. I would still have to make sure that he left town, but the hardest part was done. Now we just had to wait.

Boo's ears pricked, and she woofed softly as she sat up, staring at the item that had appeared on the table in front of us. Both of the boys were outside, digging through some of the junk out back to find the parts that they needed, so I knew that it hadn't been one of them that had snuck it in when I wasn't paying attention. Even if it had been one of them, Boo still would have let me know that someone was here. I contemplated sending her to get it, because I was pretty sure that she would be able to, but I didn't want to take the chance that there would be anything wrong with it. If it was a bomb or something magical that would prove dangerous to her, I would rather have taken care of it myself. I stood and cautiously approached the piece of paper, picking it up so that I could read it. If it had been from someone that I didn't know, I was fairly sure that it would have been in an envelope, or at the very least that it would have felt strange to me with the magic in it. The second I touched it, though, I realized why it didn't feel strange to me. This was from Mom. I can sense her magic in it, the same way I had been able to sense the magic in the notes that she had left for me in the house. It seemed like so long ago that she had left me those notes, but of course the more important leaving she had done was when she had left me on my own. That was what made it so strange that there was suddenly a note that was practically dripping with her magic, a note that had appeared out of nowhere, when she shouldn't have had any idea where I was. It made no sense, which made me all the more curious.

You did an amazing job trying to find me. I didn't expect you to, but I'm proud of what you can do. I love you, but please be safe. Go home.

Again there was no signature, just like the first set of notes. I studied it, not at all surprised that Mom had somehow managed to find me, even though she should never have been able to do that. If there was anything that this whole experience had taught me, it was that I should never underestimate what another witch was capable of, especially since I of all people knew that things could get really squirrelly in no time at all. Her magic might have allowed her to find me to send the note to me, but still, it hurt that she hadn't come herself. She said nothing of when she would be back, if she would even be coming back anytime soon. Even if I hadn't been able to find her, I had hoped that it would change her mind somehow, that she would let me join her or that it would push her to rejoin me. Instead, nothing seemed to have changed. That left me with a decision: should I stay, or should I return to the original goal and try to follow Mom? There was no reason for me to go home if she wasn't there, so I didn't even consider that. There were pros and cons to any decision that I made, but at least it was still my decision to make. This was my life, and no one got to make those choices for me. If there was anything that this experience had taught me, it was that.

I sat back down, gently stroking Boo as I thought. Mom had made it very clear that she didn't want to be found, and there was no telling what kind of trouble I could get myself into trying to change her, with the only difference from being here being that I wouldn't have the boys or Boo to help me out of it. Not that I really *needed* them, but it was less a need and more about having backup if I needed it. Besides, as much as I hated to say it, I enjoyed their company, and here was the safest that I had felt in quite some time. If I wasn't going to spend my time and energy tracking Mom down, then I might as well stay here. At least that way, when she was done, she would know where to find me.

When I looked down, Boo was looking at me, her tail wagging excitedly, so much so that her whole back end wagged. She had no idea what I was thinking, or at least I was pretty sure that she didn't, but the absolute affection in her eyes made me smile. I leaned down to kiss her between the eyes, then stood. She bounced to her feet. I had a vague idea that I might be able to ask Liam for his help in finding Mom, but I didn't know for sure that he would be able to help me. Even if he was able to help me, I wasn't ready to give up my newfound freedom, and my newfound friends, just yet. He might be able to find Mom using his powers, and if that was the case, then he would still be able to find her if I asked him later. I tried not to feel bad about asking him to find her right at this moment. She had been the one to take off and leave me, not the other way around. I wasn't sorry.

"Let's go tell the boys we'll be staying for a while. We have things to finish up here."

THE SCIENCE of Dragons
    The Journey of Dragons

AERIE of the Gryphons

KINGS AND QUEENS of War

Crystal Dark

· · ·

. . .

DARK as the Devil's Heart

ANTHOLOGIES FEATURING This Author
Airship Legends

FACEBOOK:
https://www.facebook.com/AuthorJulieKramer
Instagram: https://www.instagram.com/julie.kramer.733/
Twitter: https://twitter.com/Julie19647360
Bookbub: https://www.bookbub.com/profile/julie-l-kramer-18d1f1a8-b518-4392-9999-dd2a535f9fa7